Emanuel

or Children of the Soil

A Tale of Rural Denmark

By Henrik Pontoppidan

Illustrated by Nelly Erichsen

Published by Pantianos Classics

ISBN-13: 978-1-78987-124-1

First published in 1896

CUCKOO!

·EMANUEL·

OR·CHILDREN·OF·THE·SOIL·FROM·
THE·DANISH·OF·HENRIK·
PONTOPPIDAN·BY·MRS·
EDGAR·LUCAS·

ILLUST- BY -RATED
NELLY·ERICHSEN

IGDRASIL·

J·M·DENT·&·C⁰·ALDINE·HOUSE·LONDON·

Contents

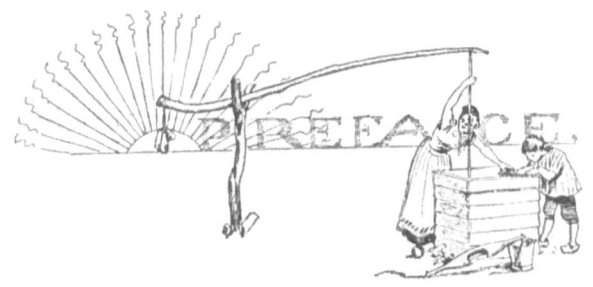

Preface

In "Emanuel, or Children of the Soil," Henrik Pontoppidan gives us a chapter in the Evolution of the Danish Peasant. The period he chooses for the story, about twenty years ago, was one filled with the falling echoes of great religious and political enthusiasms.

Until 1788, when Serfage was abolished under the regency of Frederik the Sixth, "the People's Friend," the Danish Peasant was simply a slave, bought and sold with the land he laboured on, and absolutely at the mercy of his feudal lord. Personal freedom became his then, but he was still without the other rights of a citizen. These were, however, granted him in the fullest measure by the Constitution of 1849, a constitution that was then the most free of any in Europe. This gave him, amongst other things, Religious Liberty, Manhood Suffrage, Free Education, a Free Press, and Parish Councils. The outburst of popular enthusiasm at this juncture was immense. The Peasant was half intoxicated with his new powers, and was anxious to experiment with them at once.

The two predominant political parties in Denmark at that time, under whose influence he fell, were the "National-Liberal" party and the "Friends of the Peasants." The former had grown out of the Constitutional disputes with the dependent Duchies, Schleswig and Holstein, which culminated in the war of 1848, when the Danes were victorious. It was patriotic, anti-German, Scandinavian; and taught with unmeasured enthusiasm that no personal sacrifice was too great in the cause of Denmark.

The "Friends of the Peasants" were also Patriotic, but more democratically so, and declared that the welfare of their country depended mainly on the Peasant, whom they courted and exalted in every possible way.

Both of these movements also more or less directly influenced a man who was then one of the most remarkable figures in Denmark, Bishop Nicholai Frederik Severin Grundtvig, the Saga-Priest; and through him reacted back on the Peasant. Born in 1783, he had spent his early life and manhood in combating the hide-bound orthodoxy and formal pietism of the State Church;

and by the time the Constitution was granted he had gathered a great following in the Church, and had aroused the same sort of personal enthusiasm as John Wesley in England.

He saw that the peasant, though nominally free, was still bound in ignorance, an ignorance which he bent all his mind to dispel. He had been struck during a visit to England with the efforts that were made there for the enlightenment of the poorer classes, and resolved to imitate them in Denmark.

This he did by the establishment of "High Schools" for the people, where he gathered together young men and maidens, for months at a time (the one sex in summer the other in winter), and by means of lectures, historical readings, and the singing of patriotic songs, saturated their minds with a love of their Fatherland and a knowledge of its glorious past. He put the old gods before them as the only natural and inevitable forerunners of Christianity, and constantly recited the Eddas and Sagas. The awakening of the spirit was his prime object, rather than the training of the intellect.

So successful were the High Schools that in a somewhat modified form they are now general all over Denmark, and in an address given at the opening of the new building of the Danish Students Society, in 1894, Georg Brandes said: — "If we wished to point out to a foreigner what was most remarkable in modern Denmark we should distinguish three things of National Origin," and the first of these is "the Peoples' High Schools."

This great institution, then, with its religious-political teaching, together with the outcome of the agitations of the "National-Liberal" party and the "Friends of the Peasants," form the background to the story before us. Grundtvig himself had died in 1872, but the Grundtvigians were still a united and powerful body.

The National-Liberals and the Friends of the Peasants were no longer organized parties, but they had left their mark on the minds of the People, whose keen interest in politics was kept alive by the grave dangers that loomed on the constitutional horizon. By the revision of the Constitution in 1866 their liberties were already and somewhat curtailed, and a still more serious incursion on them (to which reference is made in Mr Pontoppidan's later story, "The Promised Land," a sequel to "Emanuel") was soon to be made by the decreeing of provisionary Budgets by the King without the consent of the Rigsdag.

Veilby and Skibberup have their prototypes in two picturesque and remote villages on the Roeskilde Fjord in North Sjoelland. Here Henrik Pontoppidan lived for years, and here he learnt to know the Peasants whom he describes so charmingly, not only in "Emanuel" and "The Promised Land," but also in his volumes of short stories, "Village Pictures," and "From the Cottages." Here, too, the material for the illustrations in this volume and "The Promised Land" was collected.

Nelly Erichsen.
April 1896.

Note

In reading all names

> *a* has the sound of *a* in father
> *e* has the sound of *a* in pane.
> *i* has the sound of *ee*.
> *u* has the sound of *oo*.
> *y* has the sound of *ii*.

All final *e*'s accented, thus Hansine, Hanseené.

Book One

Chapter One

It was towards the end of the seventies.

For a week the devil's own weather had raged over the district. The storm had swept from the east on the wings of wild, jagged, blue black clouds, lashing up the waters of the fiord, so that great masses of foam were thrown high on to the fields. In many places the peasants' winter corn was completely uprooted; the reeds and rushes in the bogs were beaten down, the meadows seared, and the ditches choked with sand and earth so that the water not finding an outlet spread itself over both fields and roads. There were uprooted trees in every direction, shattered telegraph posts, broken down corn stacks, and dead birds killed by the hurricane.

In the little village of Veilby which lay quite unprotected on the top of a hill, an old barn blew down one night with such a crash, that all the people sprang up out of their beds and rushed into the street in their night clothes. A dozen chimney pots were blown down the same night, and whole flower beds uprooted in the Parsonage garden; and all the starlings' building boxes were blown out of the trees.

Nay the heavenly powers did not even spare the Provst; while the storm was at its height he stepped out one afternoon on to the verandah to look round at the scene of devastation; the wind lifted the hat from his white head, threw it to the ground like a ball, trundled it along the road, and in spite of all his efforts to stop it, swept it along in a swirling dust-cloud. It only relinquished its prey in a ditch behind some blackthorn bushes, a long way down the high road, to cast its force over a little girl who lived beyond the common, and who weeping bitterly, was struggling home from school. Then with howls and shrieks as of a hundred devils let loose, the wind enveloped the worn out little creature, puffed up her skirts and drove her nearer and nearer the edge of the road, till it at last overturned her by a corner stone, and sent her rolling with despairing cries into an old gravel pit. Here her little doubled up corpse was found next day by the searchers; a new catechism still tightly pressed to her sheltering bosom, with convulsive grasp.

Never in the memory of man had such weather been known.

"The Lord preserve those at sea," the people shouted to each other through the uproar, when they met in the street as they fought their way step by step along the road with head bowed down; or flying along with the storm behind them. "Lucky folks who have a roof over their heads," thought those who were sitting at home in their half dark rooms, where even in the middle of the day they could hardly see to read the newspaper; while the wind piped and whistled round them as if all the evil spirits were let loose on the village. The horses stood pricking up their ears in the stables, and shaking with fear; the cows bellowed one against the other as at a fire, even the cats went mewing about in a plaintive manner; and the dogs snuffed round uneasily, with their tails between their legs. When at last the storm subsided a little, the snow came tumbling down in white masses; — and though it was still early winter, the beginning of December, it remained lying on the ground and filling the ditches, hiding the uprooted trees, heaping itself against broken fences, and covering torn thatch.

For full three days and nights heaven and earth were merged in one.

By this time several people had begun to search their innermost hearts, and to make up their accounts with the Almighty in the belief that the Day of

11

Judgment must be at hand. Even on the evening of the third day when the people began shovelling away the snow drifts from the doors, and sweeping the thick cakes of snow from the window panes, more than one man standing on his door-step, in the struggling moonbeams, peering out over the desolate white waste of snow to which earth and fiord were changed, wondered "what it all meant," that is to say was it a warning, a heavenly proclamation of some great event which might be expected to befall the village, the district, or possibly the whole land in the immediate future?

Chapter Two

On the same evening a young stranger was sitting in the study with the Provst, he had arrived the day before, when the snowstorm was at its height.

He was a tall slightly built man in a long black coat and white tie. His light blue eyes looked out with an open glance, from a pale childlike face. Over his forehead, which was high and arched, waved a quantity of slightly curling hair, and a fine growth of pale down was visible on his chin and down the sides of his cheeks.

Provst Tönnesen sat opposite to him in a large old-fashioned porter's chair with earpieces and a neck cushion. He was a handsome man of giant build, with the bearing of a church dignitary; his head was massive, and covered with short bristling white hair. Behind long, overhanging, and still quite black eyebrows gleamed dark grey eyes, which together with the full curves of the nose and lips gave to the clean shaven face a somewhat southern appearance. His clothing, from the spotless cambric tie to his brocaded vest and shining boots, disclosed an unusual degree of attention to outward appearance in a village pastor. His bearing, and the way in which in the course of conversation he took whiffs from a long-stemmed pipe all revealed the self-confident man of the world.

Folding doors at his side stood open to the drawing room, a large handsomely furnished room where his daughter, a pale, auburn haired girl, sat working by a tall lamp with a green shade. Silence reigned around. All sound seemed drowned in the waste of snow without. Besides the Provst's deep bass voice only the crackling of the stove was to be heard and the monotonous chatter of a parrot in a cage by the young lady.

The young stranger was the Provst's new curate whose arrival had been awaited with much interest, not only at the Parsonage but throughout the parish. Directly after the midday meal the two priests had withdrawn to the subdued light of the study; and for the last four hours had discussed all kinds of things concerning their mutually responsible office.

The conversation was almost entirely carried on by the Provst. The curate was a very young man of six-and-twenty, and he had only a few days ago been solemnly ordained by the Bishop to the cure of souls. It was evident that he was still somewhat oppressed by his new dignity. He coloured up every time the Provst addressed him as "Herr Pastor," and looked down shyly.

The Provst began his discourse in a quiet instructive tone, dwelling somewhat on the words, as if he secretly enjoyed the unusual pleasantness of his voice, and the polish of his phrases. It did not often fall to his lot to have such an intelligent listener, and he could not resist the temptation to allow his fluency a somewhat wide range. As he came to a closer discussion of the church to-day, and when he touched upon the many controversial elements within the church his voice lost its calmness, and his language was less controlled. Finally he bent forward and said with a strong emphasis and looking straight into the curate's eyes:

"What I particularly want to impress upon you Mr Hansted is — that it is not only the priest's right, but his sacred and inalienable duty to his Master whose Kingdom on earth he administers, I say it is the undeniable duty of the priest, on every occasion to maintain the undoubted authority of the church. The beautiful old patriarchal feeling which formerly existed between the shepherd of souls and his flock will soon, unfortunately, be no more than a Saga. And whose is the blame? Who are those that for years have systematically undermined the authority of the church, and broken down the traditional respect of the people for their duly constituted ministers of religion. Are they the so-called Freethinkers, the open and audacious Atheists? It may be said that it is so, but don't believe it! No, it is within the church's own doors that the corruption has been nourished. It is those movements pregnant with disaster, which, under the name of 'democratic liberty,' and 'equality,' have risen from the dregs of the people, and which now have found their way even into the sacred precincts of the church — not only by means of hotheaded youths here and there, but — unfortunately — latterly even through some of the most trusted men in the church. I need not explain myself further, no doubt you know to what I refer. Who and what are these so-called followers of Grundtvig, — with their 'Friendly Meetings,' and their High schools, which have latterly received state support? And this 'Colporteur' nuisance, these preaching shoemakers and tailors — ignorant persons, who — mark you — are sent out by the priests themselves into the land, and empowered to bear witness in the name of the Holy Church? I cannot understand the blindness of certain of our colleagues, who do not see how destructive is such a proceeding to the dignity and authority which we (there is no use denying it among ourselves) cannot afford to be without in the presence of the common people, who are not in a position to value true superiority, or to judge rightly of spiritual qualifications. And what are the consequences? Do we not already see the fruits? These shoemaker and tailor apostles — are they not marvellous orators, almost prophets in the eyes of the populace? Their phrases and catchwords demoralize the people to such an extent, that they will hardly listen to a proper well thought out sermon, and they lose all taste for the solemnities of a church service. — It is only a few days since one of these presumptuous individuals presented himself to me as a 'colleague;'

and even had the insolence to ask permission to use the church for his ministrations! This is what we have come to! Tramps in the pulpit, criminals at the altar. In this manner is the Church's brilliance tarnished. This is what its importance has sunk to! — I ask you, Pastor Hansted, when is it to end?" He had talked himself into an ever-increasing violence of passion. His face was pale and he trembled in every limb, and at his last words he rose to his full height, straightening his giant frame as if ready for the fray at once.

The curate looked at him in astonishment and even the young lady turned her head, while the parrot screamed and flapped its wings.

Quite beside himself with excitement, the Provst tramped up and down the floor with steps which echoed through the room. In a few minutes he came back to his place, and stopping in front of the curate, looked at him with a searching glance which blazed under the dark eyebrows like lightning in a storm cloud, said, in a voice which still trembled, "I hope, Pastor Hansted, that you understand my anxiety in the case I have just mentioned; and I hope you share the doubts which every conscientious priest must entertain in the face of these movements ... I won't conceal from you that even in this parish I see traces of agitation. A certain weaver named Hansen, as ignorant as he is audacious, one of the sad products of this High school movement, has been trying, for the last year or two, to form a revolutionary party among the congregation; this party of braggarts and ignoramuses dares openly to defy me. But I won't stand it! I feel it is my duty to crush this spirit of revolt with inexorable severity, and I hope I may depend on your support in the future, Mr Hansted. I hope in all matters of importance we shall work together for the glory of God and the good of the congregation."

"I have no higher wish," answered the young man quietly, looking at the floor.

"I am quite sure of that," continued the Provst, evidently pleased by the curate's answer. "At the same time, I am glad to have it confirmed by your own lips. I do not doubt that we shall get on very well together."

At this moment a softly-chiming clock in the drawing-room struck eight. At the sound the Provst's daughter appeared in the doorway, and invited the gentlemen to come in to tea.

"Well then we must obey," said the Provst in a lively voice, and rose. Laying his hand on the curate's shoulder he added jocularly, "as you have perhaps perceived, Pastor Hansted, my daughter rules the house and I may tell you that she is a strict commander. We can continue the conversation another time. Come in, you must put up with a countrified supper table."

Chapter Three

The dining-room — like most of the Parsonage rooms — was a lofty and well-proportioned apartment, with a richly decorated ceiling and frescoes over the doors. Although Veilby and Skibberup were far from being rich livings, the Parsonage and all its out buildings were in a style more in keeping with the seat of a rich landed proprietor, than a dwelling for a servant of the church. The Provst's predecessor in the living had been an exceedingly rich man, and his first work had been to level the old Parsonage buildings with the ground. At his own cost he erected the present palatial building, the costliness of which led to pilgrimages from all parts of the country to look at it. Even now the wildest tales were told of the recklessness with which he squandered his money.

A peasant only had to go to him and complain of a misfortune with his cattle, or say that his corn was blighted, and he would immediately run a pen through his debt for tithes, and sometimes even hand him a note for 50 Daler when he left. All that he asked in return was to be left in peace with his books and his works of art; and as the parishioners always had considerably less taste for the treasures of religion than for the more tangible goods of this world, the best understanding existed between the congregation and its head during the fifteen years reign of the "Millionaire Priest."

In the meantime Provst Tönnesen complained bitterly of his predecessor, and with reason; by his proceedings he had entirely muddled the ideas of the parishioners. They had grown accustomed to regard tithes and offerings as things they might give or withhold at their discretion, so that when the Provst demanded that regularity should be re-introduced and even required strictly punctual payments, it was looked upon as unseemly greed in a priest, and gave rise to a meeting which was the first source of the strained relations which had existed ever since.

The hostile feeling against the Provst had in the last few days taken a new and characteristic turn, and it was the remembrance of this which was at the bottom of his recent violent outburst.

The fact was, that the conspiring peasants having again refused to pay their tithes, the rector had distrained, and according to a preconcerted arrangement, they had all allowed their old manure carts and wagons to be seized, and drove up one day in solemn procession before the Parsonage, where the sale was to take place. Then amid great merriment they bought their goods back again and drove off exultant.

If the Provst then had reasonable cause to be displeased with his predecessor's relations with his parishioners, he was in return doubly grateful for the princely home he had left behind him. It exactly corresponded to what, in his opinion, was a fitting residence for a Vicar of Christ in the parishes of Veilby and Skibberup; and it was partly on this account that he still held this — in proportion to his age and seniority — very moderate living. Moreover he was suffering from an imaginary mortification at the hands of the higher powers, which he attributed to the personal spite of his immediate superior, namely the Bishop, an unusually liberal minded man both in ecclesiastical affairs and in politics. It was in fact not one of Provst Tönnesen's failings to undervalue himself, and as he had more than once been passed over on the filling up of some of the larger appointments, he looked upon this as an intentional slight, and determined that he would not again apply for preferment under his present Bishop — a decision which the smallness of his family and some private fortune enabled him to maintain without any great self-denial.

He was not however, above accepting a little balm for his wound when, a year or two later he allowed himself to be nominated Provst or rural dean; a position in which he at last found a fitting field for his superfluous energy, and his self-esteem recovered from the mortifications it had undergone. From that day he lived and breathed among old documents, and acts of parliament, composing with painful solicitude sheet upon sheet of representations to diocesan authorities and county councils. He instituted elaborate enquiries at every opportunity among his subordinate clergy, and was the special dread of the school masters under his jurisdiction, whom he pursued with endless lists of reports and schedules which he insisted on having filled up with great precision. He did in fact succeed to a great extent in strengthening the clerical control over the Education Department; and it was not without reason that he considered himself at home on this subject, for in his younger days he had been assistant master at one of the public schools for several years.

He explained all these measures to the curate at the tea-table, giving him to understand that he was taking a curate so as to have more time to devote to these works.

The curate, listening in silence, absently crumbled his bread on the cloth without eating anything. He had hardly eaten at all for the twenty-four hours he had been under the Provst's roof. He did not give the impression of being ill at ease. On the contrary there was an expression of joy and thankfulness in his gentle light blue eyes, when he now and then raised them and glanced round the room, dwelling a moment on the daughter of the house, as she stood behind the steaming urn.

Miss Ragnhild Tönnesen was, like her father, a stately figure and the image of him. She had the same large expressive eyes — only a shade lighter — the same southern type of nose and well-formed mouth. But she was slim almost to thinness, nor had she inherited the Provst's healthy dark complexion. Her skin was pale and delicate, almost transparent — as if it had never known either wind or sun. On the other hand her haughty bearing and formal carriage were again quite her father's, just as the relationship could be traced in the inordinate care of her person which was disclosed by her elegant costume in the latest fashion.

Miss Ragnhild was twenty-four years old and the Provst's only child. If at the first moment she appeared somewhat older, it was the result of having been the mistress of her father's house for some years. While quite a child the Provst had lost his wife, and it was owing to the overwhelming shock of his loss that he gave up his promising future as a school master and moved into a country parsonage in search of consolation and quiet for himself and his child.

Chapter Four

They were just about to leave the table, when the lame old family servant put her head in from the kitchen, and announced that a person was at the door with a sledge, and insisted on seeing the Provst.

"At this time of day!" exclaimed the Provst, raising his eye-brows ominously, "What does he want, Loné?"

"How should I know?" she answered, sourly, "He said he had to fetch the Provst to a sick person."

"To a sick person! In this weather! And now, at night …who ever can it be, Loné?"

"How can I tell … he says he is Anders Jörgen's son from Skibberup."

"Oh, indeed!" murmured the Provst, with a gloomy look and nodding his head. "Is old Anders Jörgen to be called away now? Dear, dear? Where is the messenger?"

"I shewed him into the study."

The Provst finished his tea, wiped his mouth, and rose.

On his way through the drawing-room he drew out of his tail pocket a black silk cap, with which he was wont to cover himself before presenting himself to his parishioners. Having also prepared himself by clearing his throat loudly, he entered his study.

A little figure stood by the door in the subdued green light, enveloped in an immense great coat several sizes too large for him, from which only a light mop of hair, two swollen blue hands and a pair of feet in white woollen socks stuck out.

"Good evening," said the Provst, in a friendly voice, waving his hand, "Do you want to speak to me?"

A hiccup was his first answer, followed by "yes" in a frightened whisper.

"What is your name, friend?" continued the Provst.

For a moment the only sound was the chattering of the lad's teeth. At last the answer came hoarsely and hurriedly, "Ole Christian Julius Andersen."

"Are you a son of old Anders Jörgen of Skibberup?"

"Yes."

"Then it was you who came to me as a candidate for confirmation last year, wasn't it?"

"Yes."

"And now you have come to request me to administer the Sacrament to your old father - I thought I had heard that he had been ailing for some time."

A quiver passed through the lad at these words, he began to shift his feet uneasily and twirled his fur cap round and round in his hands like a wheel.

"It's rather late in the evening you know, and the state of the roads is very bad," continued the Provst calmly. "But in consideration of the gravity of the case I will not refuse — well, what is it? have you anything else on your mind? I suppose the roads are passable now. Are the lanes dug out?"

"Yes; but—'

"Are they cleared down under the ridge?"

"The snow clearers are out..."

"Good! go out to your horses and wait, I shall be ready directly."

With these words the Provst waved his hands again and returned to the sitting-room — without paying any attention to a pair of distracted, wide opened eyes, with which the boy followed him out of the room.

When the Provst re-entered the sitting-room and his eye fell upon the curate, who at the same moment came in from the dining-room, a smile suddenly lighted up his face.

"Listen, I have an idea," he exclaimed gaily, "I daresay you heard, Mr Hansted, that there was a message from a sick man in the parish, who wishes to receive the Holy Communion

Now, I can't think of a better opportunity than this, for you to begin your ministrations. I know the old fellow very well, he has always been a respectable hard-working man, to whom a few ordinary words of consolation will be all that is requisite. I am convinced that it will not give you the least trouble."

The Provst's request was visibly embarrassing to the young clergyman. The colour came and went quickly in his cheeks, and he began to stammer excuses. He said the Provst had promised to support him at first — till he had had some practice — besides, he was quite unprepared —.

But the Provost interrupted him hastily; "Oh, that has nothing in the world to do with it. You can think over the few words you wish to say on the way. I always do that myself, and, as I said before, a few every day words of consolation will be more than sufficient in this case. Only courage! my friend, and all will come right. The most important thing is to keep the ritual clearly in your mind and not to get confused. Go, and God be with you, dear friend, always rely surely on His blessing."

After these words the curate did not raise any more objections. He left the room quietly and went up to put on his gown.

Chapter Five

A QUARTER of an hour later the Parsonage had fallen back into its usual state of peace and quietness. Miss Ragnhild went about in the rooms putting them to rights for the night. She closed the grand piano in the corner, beneath the laurel crowned bust of Beethoven; put away the music, and kissed the sleepy parrot on the beak before covering up the cage. Then she took her accustomed seat by the table under the lamp, and went on with her work.

The Provst filled his pipe in his own room, and began wandering up and down through both rooms. Now and then he glanced somewhat nervously at his daughter, puffing out immoderately thick clouds of smoke from his pursed up lips. At last he stopped before her, and said with somewhat forced gaiety;

"Well, my little Ragnhild, what do you think of our new guest?"

The young lady's expression became cold and reserved. The question was evidently disagreeable.

"Oh! he makes a very pleasant impression," she said, indifferently.

"Yes, doesn't he? there seems to be a pleasing ingenuousness about him — a childlike freshness which is very uncommon at the present time. Now-a-days young people of twenty are already old and weary of life — I am very glad you like him, too, Ragnhild, as he is to be our daily companion."

The young lady's brow contracted.

"It would be as well not to decide too hastily on a first impression," she said, shortly. "The most important point is, whether he has the right qualities for the post — we must find that out."

"Of course, of course," exclaimed the Provst, and continued his walk. "There I quite agree with you — quite! Hm. Hallo!" he interrupted himself, as he looked at his watch, "I see it is getting late, it is time for me to get to work."

He kissed his daughter, bid her good-night, and went into his own room.

Hardly was his door closed, before the one from the kitchen opened, and the smoke-dried face of the old lame maid appeared. Finding that the young lady was alone, she crept into the room and discovering an errand by the stove, turned her head and looked anxiously at Ragnhild, with a knowing and inquisitive glance. At last she hobbled along in her stocking feet to the table where the young lady was sitting.

"Well," she said, in a whisper, slyly screwing up her eyes, "and what does my young lady think of him?"

"Of whom?" asked Ragnhild, lifting her head quickly, and looking stiffly at the old servant.

"Why, him of course — the curate!"

A lightning glance shot from Miss Ragnhild's steely grey eyes which threatened a smart storm. But thinking better of it, she repressed her anger, even forcing herself to smile, and answered quickly, and as it were, overflowing with merriment: "Yes, thank you, Lone, I am delighted with him; in fact, I am already in love with him; to-morrow I shall engage myself to him; and on Thursday we will be married. If you will come to us on Sunday week for the christening festivities, and hold our first-born at the font, my husband and I will be delighted — now, are you satisfied?"

The old servant stuck out her big chin in great offence; and with her usual scowling and sulky expression she retreated towards the door, muttering to herself.

19

Chapter Six

In the meantime the young curate was well on his way to Skibberup. The nervousness which came over him at first on the Provst's request, had quickly passed off. He was in good spirits and leant back comfortably on the wide seat, from whence he observed the winter landscape with surprise. The wind had dropped to a dead calm after sunset. The dark blue sky was brilliant with stars. In the far-distant western horizon there was still a reminiscence of the late storm, in the shape of a long bank of clouds above which rose the golden crescent of the moon.

The whole scene affected the curate like the revelation of a dream. He was a town-bred child, and only knew winter by the smoke, fog, and mud of the city. It was only a couple of days since he had been wandering about the Copenhagen streets with their inch deep mud; deafened by the rattle of cabs, the bells of the trams, and the hoarse cries of the mussel sellers — now he was sitting wrapped in the Provst's bearskin coat, gliding through fairy land, where the trees and bushes rose up from the fields like branches of white coral tinged with blue, and the sledge rushed on noiselessly with a swaying motion as if borne on long soft wings.

All at once he became violently agitated. The image of his poor dead mother rose before him, and he wished most earnestly that she could have seen him at that moment. He knew that it had been her dearest wish to live to see that day; and he felt more strongly than ever before, how entirely it was owing to her that he had found courage to follow the call to the ministry of the Holy Word.

And how grateful he was to her for it!

It was no good now for his father, the Etatsraad, to shake his head at his "wild ideas." The die was cast! His gay brother, a lieutenant in the guards, shortly to be "Kammeryunker," might for the future save himself the trouble of turning down a side street, for fear of meeting him in a hat which did not come up to the latest fashion; or with a friend who was not in "Society." And his good little sister, wife of a consul-general, would no longer need to shed tears at his want of social tone and polished manners — Emanuel was gone, the theological student was out of the way, and he would certainly not be quick to return.

No indeed, he would not turn back.

He looked around on the far-stretching shimmering snowfields with great content, and he felt as if he had climbed up from a deep, dark well, to a land very near heaven.

Here and there among the fields a reddish glimmer was to be seen from the lights in the cottage windows, which twinkled like fallen stars. An unearthly peace rested over the whole face of nature. No other sound was to be heard under the dome of heaven than the horses' rusty little bells; but in the intense stillness, this tinkling was like an echo of a thousand voices, as if the air was full of invisible bells.

He fell into a reverie — this then was henceforth to be his home, he was to wander through these fields, and to go into these cottages as the chosen servant of the Lord! — he already saw himself sitting in these small, low-roofed houses among the poorly clad, listening men and women, and he felt how dearly he would love them, how in the most miserable cabin — yes, there especially — he would be a hundred times happier than he had ever been in his father's magnificent house

He was so full of these thoughts that he did not notice how the youth, his driver, several times turned half round towards him, as if about to speak and then ducked down quickly into his big mantle again as if he did not dare. But suddenly he was aroused by a loud shout from many voices just in front of them. The sledge was in a deep lane where the snow had gathered in such drifts that the horses could only go at a walking pace between the wall of snow, a yard high, which had been thrown up on both sides. The driver immediately stopped the horses, and in the faint light cast by the last corner of the moon which still peeped up above the cloud bank in the west, the curate saw, fifty yards ahead of them, a party of snow clearers hard at work. Somewhat nearer, only a dozen paces off, stood another group of men resting on their shovels, and it was they who had recognized the Provst's chair, [1] and therefore shouted out:

"Ye'll have to stop a bit whoever ye are — can't ye see the snow's slippin here? — we'll have it cleared in a minnit — who are ye then?"

"I am the clergyman," called back the curate, somewhat shyly, it was the first time he had called himself by his new title aloud. "We are on our way to a sick person."

The sound of his voice made the men start.

They all looked up at once and put their heads together, whispering to each other. At last one of them went forward and began talking to the driver in an undertone; the excitement soon spread to the whole party. Slowly, and as if with anxious curiosity, they approached the sledge from both sides. Most of the men were short and strongly built, with broad smiling faces, their eyes glittering like fishes' scales in their red faces. Some waddled forward in big sea boots, others had wooden shoes and long white woollen stockings drawn up over the trousers far above the knees. Most of them wore big fur caps with flaps tied over the ears, and one had on a sou'wester.

The curate felt somewhat uneasy on suddenly seeing himself surrounded by a troup of inquisitive, staring people. Should he speak to them? They were evidently his parishioners. Then a tall black-bearded man stepped forward — a giant to look at among the others, and plainly the one who was accustomed to be spokesman. He drew a big mitten off his right hand with his strong white teeth, and said with a powerful voice:

"Beg pardon, we're villagers from Skibberup, and we hear you're the new curate - ye must e'en give us leave to bid ye welcome. Welcome Pastor

21

Hansted."

Then the others came quickly forward — and before the curate had time to collect himself, he saw himself encompassed by half a score of big red fists, which were stretched towards him with a hearty "Welcome."

For a moment he was quite confused. He felt he must say something, and also perceived that the men expected it. But it had come upon him so unexpectedly that he could find nothing to say beyond repeating, "Thank you, thank you," while he cordially pressed the out-stretched hands.

EMANUEL INTRODUCED TO HIS PARISHIONERS.

Just then the clearers in front shouted that the way was open. The driver shook the reins and the sledge began to move. At the last moment he found words and said, "Good-bye friends — thank you for your welcome! I shall consider myself lucky if I always find such men to clear the way for me! I hope we shall get on well with each other!"

"That we will, never fear!" was answered back from many mouths.

"And we hae need to!" shouted a deep threatening voice at the back of the group, followed by a murmur of approbation.

These words and the tone in which they were spoken startled the curate. While the sledge flew over the snow he mused in astonishment over the meaning of the man's words. He pondered upon it so long, that the sledge reached Skibberup before he had an idea they were so near. At the sight of the first house he started up in dismay — all this time he had entirely forgotten the sick man, and didn't know in the least what he was to say to him. But he soon re-assured himself. The meeting with the snow clearers had given him confidence, and he did not doubt, that at the decisive moment, the Lord would put the right words into his mouth.

[1] The clergy and doctors have a large armchair which is slung in the sledge or wagon, which always has to be sent for them in the country when their services are required.

Chapter Seven

SKIBBERUP lay in a hollow surrounded by high hills which only open out on the east, towards the near lying fiord. The curate was at once struck by the number of small houses, and shabby little farms of which the village consisted. There was hardly a single large holding to be seen, but there were about fifty cottages clustered round a large pond, which reflected the starry sky in its dark waters amidst the snow. They were grouped picturesquely under the hills, some nestling on the slopes like a "saeter village," round a mountain tarn. Moreover, the village was half hidden by enormous masses of snow, which had been driven in from the fiord. Only the top ridge and smoke blackened chimney of many of the cottages were visible. A glimmer of light was still shining from a few windows, and an old man stood on one of the doorsteps, resting on a crutch, and waving his cap gaily as they swept by.

The sledge stopped outside a small farm which lay a little way off the road in the southern outskirts. The tarred gates were open, and a dim lantern hung in the archway, turning slowly round at the end of a cord. The curate had to alight under this lantern, for the courtyard was so packed with snow, that the sledge couldn't go any further. He walked up a narrow path which had been cleared, through the drifts to a low dwelling house.

A dead silence reigned. Only the faint rattle of a chain was to be heard in the stable, and somewhere behind a wall a cat mewed. When he got to the entrance he heard a door open inside, and a soft woman's voice said quietly, "I thought I heard bells — th' Provst must hae come." He knocked at the door, and the next moment he found himself in a long, low room, with old-fashioned furniture, small windows, a timbered ceiling, and dark earthen floor. A thin tallow candle with a flaring wick, was burning on one end of a heavy oaken table, and, at his entrance, a little, middle-aged man got up. He had a shock head of iron-gray hair, and a pair of rusty brass spectacles were resting on a broad thick nose. The man had been reading a paper, which he now — visibly flustered — hastened to hide under the table, and, at the same moment, remembering his spectacles, he tore them off with embarrassment, as if he had been caught in some piece of folly.

As he was about to approach the expected Provst, he fell back in amazement, and stared open-mouthed at the stranger, who remained standing by the door, greeting him in a friendly voice.

"Pray, don't be alarmed," said the curate as he advanced. "I am the Provst's representative, his curate — and come to you by his request."

At this moment the door of an adjoining room was cautiously opened, and a heavily built, middle aged woman with iron-gray hair and large, prominent eyes came in. She also stopped in mute astonishment, and, for a moment, measured the strange clergyman with a not very friendly glance But suddenly a bright cheery smile lit up her face, and approaching the curate without any awkwardness, she offered him her fleshy hand, and said in a remarkably soft, childlike voice —

"It's surely never our new curate? ...Nay then you're heartily welcome! ... So you've really come at last! I'd never expected such a piece of luck...Well I am glad, that I am! ... So you're really the new priest, and this is what you look like! It's just what I might have expected...I'm right down glad to see you and no mistake!"

She planted herself in front of him a little way off with her hands folded on her big stomach, and continued her outbursts of delight, while she eyed him from head to foot.

The curate, after a time, began to feel this inspection somewhat embarrassing, and asked after the sick person.

But she could not get over her joyous surprise, or tear herself away from her observation of him. Only when her husband anxiously pulled her skirt once or twice, from behind, did she answer the curate's enquiries.

"Oh, thank ye," she said, in a changed voice, looking towards the door, which she had left ajar behind her: "The Lord be thanked! There's a change for the better, but in the middle of the day she was cruel bad, an when the weather mended, we thought it as well to send a message to the Provst; may be we'd better have left it alone, now the danger's over, an it's no treat for the priest to come out o' nights with such bad roads."

"Oh don't think about that," the curate interrupted her; "there is nothing to be said on that account. You must send for me whenever you want me, I shall always be at your service. Don't you think, if all is ready in the patient's room, that we had better go in?"

The woman carefully opened the door of the side room, and all three stepped quietly down into an oblong, dimly lighted room, a step lower than the living room. A little table with a shaded lamp, a medicine bottle, and a prayerbook, stood at the head of a broad bed which took up the narrow wall. In the bed lay a brown-haired girl, with heavy, closed eyelids, and a dark fever flush on her cheek.

The young priest turned round hastily, and said in bewilderment:

"But what is this?"

"It is our daughter," answered the woman, looking at him in astonishment.

"What? ...But the Provst said..." The curate began to stammer. In his shyness he kept his back to the bed, for the young girl lay peasant fashion, only in her chemise, and in her fever had thrown both her bare arms outside the quilt.

"But it was an elderly man who was ill...

The Provst said...Let me see — wasn't his name Anders Jörgen?"

"Me!" burst out the man on hearing his name, and looked up confusedly with his small half blind eyes. "I'm beholden to ye for th' inquiry, but I'm all right."

"But then it is altogether a misunderstanding. ..."

"Yes, it is our daughter Hansine," continued the woman quietly, and then she began to relate how the illness came on three days ago, with pains in the back and loins. At first they didn't think anything of it; but the pains went into the neck, and the night before, their daughter suddenly became so much worse that they had to send for the doctor. When he came, he shook his head, and even at mid-day he said it might turn to anything...But now he thought the worst was over.

During this history the curate had time to recover somewhat from his first surprise. He was even a little ashamed of his perturbation; and forcing himself to concentrate his thoughts on the sacred rite he was about to administer, he approached the bed again.

At that moment the patient woke up, and opening her dark blue eyes, fixed them in feverish delirium on the stranger, with a rigid and reluctant expression. Her mother bent over her and told her who it was, ...and then the young girl drew a long sigh of relief, and closed her eyes quietly, as much as to say she had been longing for this and was prepared.

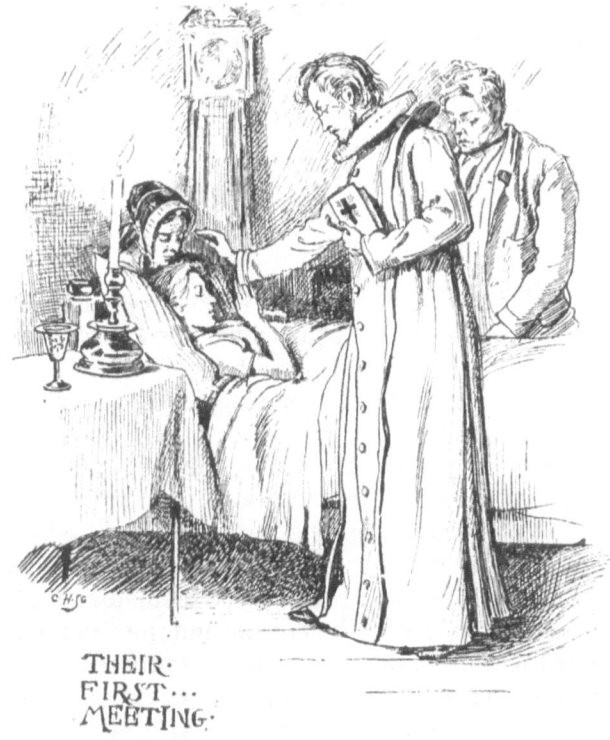

THEIR·
FIRST···
MEETING·

Her mother carefully put the wadded quilt to rights about her, took the prayer-book from the table, and sat down on the chair at the head of the bed, to be at hand to help her when she had to take the cup. The old father solemnly took his stand at the foot of the bed; and at the last moment the light-haired boy crept fearfully in at the door, where he remained leaning against the doorpost, his lips quivering with suppressed crying. He stared uninterruptedly at the Sacramental Bread, and the little silver chalice, which, in the meantime, the curate had taken out of the case, and placed upon the table under the lamp.

All was reverently hushed. The only sound was the loud ticking of the tall old clock in the corner, and the laboured breathing of the patient.

The young priest stepped to the bedside, and folded his hands to pray.

But whether the sight of the young girl, or the agitation he was thrown into by the sacred office ... or perhaps the sudden change from the fresh, frosty air to the close sick room, was the cause, ... his brain refused to put a single sentence together. A curious dizziness came over him, his tongue was glued to the roof of his mouth, and he felt a cold sweat breaking out on his forehead.

Then all at once a verse, an evening hymn, which his mother had taught him as a child, flashed across his mind. He had not thought of it for many years, now it came to him like an angel from heaven. He had a sensation as if some one were standing at his side, and taking him by the hand. Almost like listening to a stranger, he heard himself speaking fervent and heartfelt words, about the grace of God, the all-goodness of God, and the death of Jesus Christ for the sins of mankind.

Even the well-known sentences of the ritual became new and living in his mouth; and when at last he laid his hand on the girl's forehead to give the absolution, all his trembling soul was penetrated with the feeling that at this moment God's strengthening spirit was being imparted through him.

Chapter Eight

The same night four persons were playing cards in the sky-blue best parlour of Jensen, the chairman of the Parish Council.

They were — besides the host — Aggerbölle the district veterinary surgeon, the old schoolmaster Mortensen, and Villing the shop-keeper. They all belonged to Veilby.

They had been sitting round the same table since ten o'clock in the morning, without other interruptions than those required for meals. The clock now pointed to three. The candles had twice burnt down to the sockets, and four times in the course of the evening had hot water for toddy been brought in from the kitchen. No one yet seemed to think of breaking up the party, though the fumes of the cognac and the smoke from the glowing stove, combined with the thick blue clouds of tobacco which rendered them almost invisible to each other, had considerably cooled their ardour.

Not an unnecessary word was uttered. Half mechanically the cards were thrown on the table, and the tricks taken up. Even little Villing's goggle eyes, which usually were busy enough spying out the cards of the other players, were now blood-shot and starting out of his head like a boiled haddock's; in fact the game only went on because no one had resolution enough to bring it to a close. The only one who still kept up valiantly was the old schoolmaster. But he might have been born at an Ombre table.

From the moment that he carefully spread out his coat tails on taking his seat, till he was plainly informed that the game was over, he sat holding his venerable white head as erect as possible, hiding the fever he was always thrown into at the sight of cards and money, under an immoveably grave mask; while only an irrepressible trembling of the lips and the continual creaking of his stiff old boots betrayed his excitement. Now and then, at critical moments, he wiped the pearling sweat from his forehead with a red silk handkerchief; and if, after careful consideration, he ventured to "ask for cards," he would shut his eyes as if breathing a mental prayer. Jensen, the host, sat on his right, struggling in vain with sleep. He was a big stout peasant with a fiery red face and a drooping purple nose. He was the rich man of the neighbourhood, and his whole bearing and attire showed that he considered himself something more than an ordinary peasant. His friends used to call him "Squire Jensen," or Mr Jensen without the christian name. In return he allowed them to fleece him as much as they liked, nay, he even burst into roars of laughter every time he had to produce a fresh "krone" from his trousers pockets. He was not specially interested in the game, although he was proud of having learnt this aristocratic "Lummer" which was played in gentlemen's houses. He was also flattered by the greedy coveting of his money by the others, and he flung the coins to them as if he were feeding a herd of swine.

Aggerbölle, the vet., sat opposite the schoolmaster — he was a powerful broad-shouldered man with thick brown hair and a grizzled beard. He sat resting his head on his hand, buried in a dull, gloomy reverie. Now and then he ran his hand through his bushy mane, beating his forehead and cursing himself bitterly. The toddy had gone to his head, and he had been very unlucky this evening. Only a vanishing number of Jensen's coins had found their way to his pocket — and for Aggerbölle, card-playing was not a mere pastime, as it was to the others, — it was a life and death struggle for existence.

Suddenly the schoolmaster's old boots began to creak violently under the table. His eyes, under their silvery brows, turned anxiously towards a saucer of 25 öre pieces which stood in the middle of the table, the so-called "Pool."

At last he wiped his pale face, closed his eyes for a moment as he did on Sundays before saying the opening prayer at the chancel steps, and said quietly, "I play for the pool!"

The drowsy figures started up, and the vet. lifted his heavy head, ready to cry with exasperation.

"What suit?" he growled.

"Clubs," answered the schoolmaster benignly.

The cards were brought in silence. The vet. pulled himself together for the fray, sipped his toddy and stroked his beard with his hairy hand. His eyes were as red as a bull's. He would try one more tilt with fortune. If this solo were won, the game would come to an end, and with it all hope for this evening. Mortensen had three "Matadors," and a four of trumps, besides the king, queen, and three of hearts, and two small spades. He also had the lead. Like a

27

careful general he kept his king of hearts back, and sent the queen into the fire first.

The vet, who could not follow suit, was not to be imposed upon.

"That's a blind, I expect," he growled, and took it with a trump.

The first drops of sweat made their appearance on Mortensen's forehead.

The vet. played a small trump, Villing took it with the king; Mortensen had to follow suit. Then hearts appeared again from Villing, Mortensen followed suit with his king, the vet. took it with a trump and played his queen of spades.

Now Mortensen saw that he was lost, his boots ceased creaking, and he turned as white as a sheet. Then unnoticed, he dropped the small spade with which he ought to have followed suit into his lap, whence it slid between his knees on to the floor, where he quickly put his foot on it, at the same time taking the queen with a small trump. Then he threw his three Matadors on to the table in rapid succession, so as to have an opportunity of replacing the missing card from one of his tricks; and in the general fog no one noticed that the six of trumps from the first trick re-appeared in the sixth.

The schoolmaster won his "Solo" and the game came to an end at last.

Just then the richly gilt clock on the chiffonier struck four admonitory strokes. With a righteous smile Mortensen collected his evenly piled heaps of money into an old-fashioned leather purse and buried it in the bottom of his deep trousers pocket, carefully buttoning it up.

At this moment the host's deformed little wife appeared at the door of the adjoining room; she had been sitting wrapped in a big shawl and dozing by the kitchen fire. With an almost inaudible voice, which she tried to make grand, and with an awkward movement of her withered hand, she invited the gentlemen to come in to a "little refreshment."

The host rose too, repeating the invitation in his noisy way. "C-come in, come in and have a l-little refreshment — we n-need something to eat after our labours!"

The "little refreshment," which was served in the next room, turned out to be a fully laid table with pickled pork, ham, sausages, poached eggs, goose, liver pie, and various smoked meats, besides a first course of hot steak and onions; in addition there was a plentiful supply of corn brandy and Bavarian beer. Although the guests had partaken of four solid meals at the same table in the course of the day and night, they attacked the food with good-will, and soon emptied both the decanter of brandy and the well-filled dishes. At the end of the meal, coffee was served with cognac.

In the middle of the meal the vet. broke out into a tremendous oath, and banged his glass on to the table so hard that the stem broke. He had suddenly remembered a sick cow he had promised to see in a neighbouring village, and to which he had been on the way when he dropped in at the parish councillor's in the morning.

Jensen, unfortunately, immediately on his arrival, proposed to send a message to the schoolmaster and the shopkeeper to come and have a game of cards; and as Aggerbölle was very hard up for a few kroner to pay his baker's bill, he had allowed himself to be talked over, in the hope that in a few hours he might win what he wanted. In the course of the game the sick cow as well as everything else went clean out of his head. This was by no means of rare occurrence with Aggerbölle. Every morning he left his home in a tiny, mud-bespattered gig, solemnly promising himself and his wife that he would visit all his patients. Seldom did he get further than the first farm where there was a prospect of cards and of winning some ready money. His life was a continuous wild chase after one or two ten-kroner notes which he must find within four-and-twenty hours to pay the baker or the shoemaker. As the visits to patients were not paid on the spot; he could never withstand the temptation to try and get out of his difficulties by a bold dip into fortune's purse. He had now fallen into a complete state of imbecility. Without knowing what he was doing, he drained glass after glass, and at last sank back with open mouth, and only woke up when the little shopkeeper laid his hand on his shoulder and said: "Come, Aggerbölle, it's five o'clock."

Chapter Nine

After Mortensen had got into his soft feather bed at home, he folded his hands on the counterpane, and said the Lord's Prayer.

His wife lay by his side, and as she turned round, half awake, the bed creaked under her large weighty person.

"Did you win anything, Mortensen?"

He continued his prayer undisturbed, and said at the end:

"Twelve kroner, my dear!" whereupon he fell softly and peacefully asleep.

In the meantime Villing had also reached his shop, which was in the middle of the village, near the pond. He walked along half asleep, but when he entered the shop and perceived the well-known mixed odour of soap, raisins, coffee, and tobacco, he became wide awake at once. He stopped a minute in the dark listening to the heavy snoring of the shop boy in a little closet at the back of the shop. Then he lighted a candle end which stood ready for him on the counter, noiselessly counted the change in the till, inspected the boxes of raisins and prunes, peered up into the rafters, and held the candle down into the cellar; and only when he had satisfied himself that there was nothing suspicious to be seen anywhere did he go into the bedroom.

His young wife sat up in bed rubbing her eyes, and at once began a minute statement of all that had taken place in the shop during the day; the miller who had been there with grain, Hans Jensen who had bought a cask of brandy, and Soren, the old tailor, to whom she had given credit for a pound of candy — and so on. She was a plump little creature with a round childish face framed in a big grandmother's nightcap.

Villing undressed rapidly, throwing in approving remarks. "Good! — very good, little Sine — very well done, little friend," he ejaculated from time to time as he skipped about in his socks and drawers, looking as if he was chasing his own shadow, which now shrunk up like a frog in one corner, and then spread out like a ghost on the low walls of the little room.

For a long time after the light was put out they talked under the clothes about the prices of coffee, meal, and credit. Even in their tenderest moments these two prudent persons never forgot their business for a moment.

Aggerbölle was the one of the three wanderers who had furthest to go.

He lived in a little neglected house half a mile from the village, on the way to the shore. Fifteen years ago — when, newly married, he came to this neighbourhood — he chose this desolate place on purpose to enjoy his happiness in solitude. There was a wide view of the Fiord and the shore from the windows. Many a balmy spring evening and moonlight autumn night he and his young wife had wandered among the silent hills, arm in arm, cheek pressed to cheek, while their hearts beat with joy and lightsome hope.

Now, he many a time swore at the distance, as, dazed with drink and play, he stumbled home in the dark through mire and snow. His gig was generally left at the place where he had stranded in the day; for when it came to going home, he was usually in no state to be trusted with a horse. Nor would Jensen, this evening, hand over his vehicle, although with the snow on the ground it was quite light, and the road was cleared nearly all the way to his house. But Aggerbölle did not keep to the road, he floundered across the fields in great circles, over his top boots in snow, stopping every moment with loud lamentations, beating his forehead with his fist and cursing himself and all the world. Never — he thought — had fate been so hard upon him as to-day, and never — so he fancied — had he loved his wife and children so dearly as now, when all ways were closed to him. In the morning the baker would bring his bill for the third time, he had already been threatened with the bailiff and a summons. How should he find a way out of it? He hardly owned a halter to hang himself with! — He stopped again in a great snow-drift, unbuttoned his coat, and took a few small coins from his waistcoat pocket with his swollen fingers, and held them in the hollow of his hand. He stood a moment counting them carefully, and then, with a loud sobbing sigh, clenched his hands and started again.

When at length he reached his home, and found the gate in the tumble-down fence, fear and shame — as they always did — made him for the moment perfectly sober. He took off his heavy boots in the passage, and crept softly in his stocking feet into the bedroom. It was crowded with children's beds, and a night-light was burning on a chair by his wife's bed.

He gave a sigh of relief. His wife's eyes were closed, her thin hand was folded under her pale cheek, and she seemed to be sound asleep. But hardly had he begun to undress, than he heard her move her head, and when he looked round he met a glance from her large, brown eyes, whose brightness betrayed that for her, too, the night had brought no sleep.

"Good — good night, little Sophie!" he hiccupped tenderly, supporting himself against the bed-post.

"Good morning," she answered quietly.

"Ah well, yes," he replied with an attempt at gaiety. "It certainly is rather late — or early — Ah! — It's that Mortensen, you know — he's a regular dog at a card table — a regular dog."

She did not answer him, but closed her eyes wearily, then opened them again and said:

"A messenger on horseback came from Anders Jensen of Egede. It seems you had promised to go and look at a sick cow there."

"I?" he burst out, colouring up and trying to look her straight in the face. "I know nothing about it — it must be a mistake."

She continued calmly, "The messenger was to say that it did not matter now for the cow was dead. But you were not to trouble yourself to go there again."

Aggerbölle was silent. He stood leaning against the bedpost looking at the floor — the swollen blue veins standing out on his forehead, and his lips compressed.

All at once he drew himself up with a shiver, ran his hand through his hair, and walked with a firm step up to his wife with his right hand outstretched.

"Here you have my hand, Sophie, it is the last night I will touch a card — I swear to you that from this day I will become another man. Do you hear, Sophie? — you may depend upon me — you must trust me this time," he went on, repeating, while his tears began to flow. "I swear to you it will all come right. And I will make up to you, Sophie, for all the bad times — for all that you have suffered for my sake — for the children's sake — for Oh, God — oh, God!"

The intoxication had come over him again. He sank on his knees by his wife's bed, and buried his head in the clothes like a child, while terrible sobs shook his heavy frame.

She lay quite still for a moment with closed eyes. Then she lifted her languid hand from the counterpane and stroked his hair — she could not help it, although she had heard the same repentant weeping hundreds of times before, and had let herself be deceived by the same solemn promises. At last her eyes filled with tears too, and clasping his head with both her hands, she pressed it to her emaciated bosom, and whispered: "My poor — poor Bernhard!"

·BOOK· ·TWO·

Book Two

Chapter One

Skibberup Church lay nearly a mile from Skibberup village — on the top of a bare, solitary hill, which jutted out into the Fiord. "Kirkness" was joined to the mainland by a low, narrow neck of land, on which only a little pale grass, heather, and a creeping thorn grew, among the sand and stones. The church itself was a very ancient and much dilapidated structure of rough hewn stone, with a brick tower of later date. The whole place made an uncanny impression from its desolation. Round about among the weather-beaten graves were strewn broken tiles, fragments of chalk, and bits of glass; and on entering the church one was met by an icy chill from the bare white-washed walls, which even in summer were green with damp. In winter the cold was so intense that the water in the font froze to solid ice, and the priest had to wear overshoes and thick mittens in the pulpit.

On week-days the church remained undisturbed except for the visits of the tall lean sexton, who went by the name of "Death." He used to wander out from the village, morning and evening, meditatively, with his long bony arms crossed behind his back, to ring out a few deep notes from the rusty bells, over the foxes prowling among the thorns, the parish clerk's sheep grazing sadly outside the churchyard walls, or, now and then, over a solitary fisher-man catching bait in his boat under the steep cliffs.

But on Sundays — especially the great festivals — all was life and bustle. Then the road from Skibberup swarmed with pedestrians in holiday clothes and well-cleaned vehicles. The fishermen came sailing round the "Ness" and lay to by the big stone on the beach, whence the men carried the women ashore. The women all wore black church-going hoods, and many carried wreaths and crosses of moss and flowers, which they laid on the wind-swept graves, before going into church in single file. In the meantime "Death" stood at his look-out post, at one corner of the churchyard, whence he could see the clergyman's carriage coming along the Veilby road. As soon as he caught a glimpse of the hood among the hills, he hurried with his long strides across the graves into the tower; and while the men who had assembled in groups, talking outside the church door, slowly filed in and took their seats under the echoing arches, with much devout coughing and sniffing, the bells in the tower pealed out so lustily that all the walls shook.

But this was all a half-forgotten tale. Since Provst Tönnesen had come to the parish, the church had many a time stood empty even on Sundays; the rusty bells had pealed over deserted roads, and the only ones there to cough had been a few debtors for tithes, who dared not rouse the Provst's anger. And after all, it was by the Provst's directions that a stove had been placed in the church some few years ago, and the pews carpeted with thick rush matting.

But it was in the village of Skibberup that the revolutionary party were specially strong, and it was there also that Hansen, the notorious weaver, had his headquarters. The sight of the empty benches made Provst Tönnesen furious every Sunday. On one occasion he worked himself up into such a passion, and brought his hand down with such force on the pulpit, that St Peter, who, with the other apostles, was carved in wood on the sides of it, lost both nose and mouth from the shock. Since Pastor Hansted came to the parish, a change had taken place, and one Sunday in the end of March — the first spring-day — the sound of many voices again floated over the Fiord and mingled with the shriek of the gulls flying near the shore.

On the road by the churchyard wall a long row of conveyances with shining horses stood waiting for the service to come to an end. Some of the drivers sat on the seats half-asleep, resting their heads on their hands. Others lay in the ditches passing the time in smoking and gossip.

The Provst's hooded carriage was standing in front, by the gate, with the driver on the high box seat; he was an old-womanish sort of man in a big blue greatcoat.

The waiting lads were in the habit of poking fun at him, "Maren," as he was generally called, after his deceased wife, to whom in return (and not without reason) they had given his christian name, Rasmus. To-day, as usual, four or five lively fellows stood round with their hands in their pockets laughing at him.

"A' say, Maren!" said one of them, winking slyly, "whaat's it comin' to wi' the curate an' your young leddy? A' think they've looked long enough at one another to ha' made it oop be now!"

"A'll tell thee what," said another who was leaning carelessly against the gate-post. "It does na go so fast among fine folks; these ere young leddies are just like the hens — they allus hae to wriggle their tails a bit afore they gie theirsels oop. Isn't it true what a' say, Maren?"

The man sat immoveable on his box and did not answer. He thought it quite beneath his semi-clerical position to join in the gossip of such blasphemers who made fun of the Provst's coachman, and took Miss Ragnhild's name in vain.

At this moment the hymn came to an end in the church, the porch-door opened and the people streamed out.

Among the men who had been assembling by the entrance to await the parish meeting was one who was the object of unusual attention on all sides. He was a middle-aged man, in peasant's clothing, tall, thin, and somewhat bent, with long drooping arms and a remarkably small, flat head. His face was of a peculiar feline type, clever and alert, with small, red-rimmed eyes, and a thin red beard.

Most of the men went up to him with outstretched hand, and an enquiring glance, which he regularly answered by drawing up his mouth to a distorted smile, and drooping one eyelid.

Suddenly the cluster of people divided, and Pastor Hansted appeared in his gown and ruff.

Although he had preached several times before, both here and at Veilby, he looked pale and fatigued, and greeted the assembled people with visible embarrassment; they also uncovered somewhat unwillingly. The man with the cat's face did not touch his hat at all but remained standing, with his lip curled, while he followed the figure of the young priest with a contemptuous glance to the door of the carriage, where "Death" stood with his hat in his hand, bending to the dust like a worm.

As soon as the old coachman had set the horses going, the curate sank back in the corner of the carriage and pressed his hand to his forehead with an expression of pain. He threw his soft, wide-brimmed hat into the seat at once, as if it burnt his forehead; and as the carriage jolted and creaked along the uneven road, he remained for several minutes with closed eyes and compressed lips, as if he could hardly keep back his tears.

Chapter Two

HE was received in the Parsonage by the Provst, who had just returned from the service in Veilby church. The arrangement between the two clergymen was, that they both preached every Sunday, one at Skibberup, the other at Veilby. This was a device of the Provst's, for he feared, and not without reason, that the badly disposed villagers of Skibberup, who so stubbornly declined his ministrations, would further shew their enmity by flocking to the church when the curate preached. Therefore he only made known at the last moment at which church he himself would officiate; and in consequence, for some time, both churches were crowded, everybody hoping to hear the new priest.

Refreshed by the sight of his faithful Veilby adherents, the Provst came back in a cheerful mood, and sat down to the luncheon table with a capital appetite. An entertainment which was to take place in the evening, and for which preparations had been going on for some days, also contributed to his good humour. In general the Provst and his daughter lived very quietly, as they never took part in the festivities of the peasants, and but seldom in those of the few, and far from well-to-do Squires of the neighbourhood. But twice a year the Provst gave, — as it were, an official dinner — to which representatives of the different classes in the congregation were "commanded," almost in the same sense as to the table of royalty.

The Provst always conducted the preparations for these entertainments himself. He had a perfect passion for managing, ordering, and giving directions. He had already, some days before, given orders for the purchase of wine, meat, and various delicacies; and no sooner had he seated himself at the table and arranged his napkin under his chin, than he began to give his daughter the most minute directions about the temperature of the wines and the preparation of the salads.

In the meantime the curate sat silent, absently crumbling his bread in his usual manner and eating next to nothing. His appearance had perceptibly changed in the course of the winter. His cheeks had grown hollow, and his once clear, frank eyes were clouded over and betrayed the canker gnawing at his heart.

Miss Ragnhild looked at him several times from the other side of the table with an observant eye. Under pretext of work for the evening festivity, she had not, according to her usual custom, accompanied her father to church, and was still dressed in a flowered morning gown of soft warm stuff, with a long pointed bodice and big puffed sleeves. There was an expression of hidden anxiety on her transparent face and large blue gray eyes, as well as sisterly sympathy with the curate's troubles, which she seemed to know and understand.

At last even the Provst noticed that Mr Hansted was more than usually absent-minded, and when, suddenly addressing a question to him, he received a confused answer, he wrinkled his forehead disapprovingly. He did not think it suitable that his curate should be inattentive when he spoke, even if it was only about pies and salads. Altogether the Provst was not nearly so pleased with his curate as at one time he had expected to be. He felt himself oppressed by this person who became more peculiar and reserved every day, and went about his house evidently the prey of some secret trouble. He could not imagine what was weighing upon him, feeling satisfied that both he and his daughter did all in their power to make his stay with them as pleasant and home-like as possible. In particular he felt unpleasantly affected by the curate's demeanour towards Ragnhild. He could not be blind to the fact that there was an understanding between the two, and he thought he had grounds for believing that Mr Hansted was not indifferent to his daughter. But so far the curate had not taken any decisive step. The Provst did not know if fickleness was the cause, or excessive shyness, but in either case it seemed to him that he had a right to be aggrieved.

If, notwithstanding this, he had hitherto kept his impatience in check, it was entirely out of regard for Ragnhild, whose solitariness and unsecured future often caused him much uneasiness. On this occasion he again choked back his exasperation — only by great self-restraint. But no sooner had they risen from the luncheon table, and the curate had gone up to his room, than he eased his mind.

"I can't understand that man!" he broke out, beginning to pace hurriedly up and down the room. "I can't imagine what he has on his mind. He sits here with us every day, silent and unsympathetic, as if he were overwhelmed by some great misfortune! Do you know what can be the reason, Ragnhild?"

"Oh," answered his daughter, quietly — she had remained at the table leaning against the back of the chair, looking out of the window with thoughtful and half-closed eyes — "I suppose it would not be so extraordinary if he felt somewhat oppressed by his office at first. He is so young — and besides, he has perhaps perceived that his sermons have not won the unmixed approval of the people."

"Oh, so far as that goes, he need not reproach himself," answered the Provst, with a feeling of complacency. "And I don't believe it's anything of that sort that's troubling him. In that case he would certainly have come to me with his troubles. No, I'm afraid he doesn't understand himself. There's something wavering about him. Perhaps he's got some crotchet or other about himself in his head. That sort of thing runs in the family, I hear. His mother — according to what Pastor Petersen tells me — was a highly eccentric person, who eventually took her own life in a fit of temporary insanity."

Miss Ragnhild turned to her father with a startled glance.

"What do you say! — his mother!"

The Provst stopped and cleared his throat. In his eagerness, and by a slip of the tongue, he had mentioned a subject on which he had resolved to keep silence for the sake of the curate and the congregation.

"Well, — I don't know exactly, of course!" he said, as with a reassuring smile and wave of the hand he resumed his walk. "People say as much — I only mean, that our good Mr Hansted has too great an inclination to be wrapped up in himself, a want of the power of assimilating himself; but I know I have done all I could to make him feel at home. And I am sure you have, too. I've often seen you walking in the garden together. You have — as far as I understand — many tastes in common; he thinks a great deal of your music — he told me so himself! So I can't imagine what makes him so reserved — for I don't suppose that you, Ragnhild — in any way — have — have hurt him?"

The Provst stopped again, this time in a dark corner of the room — and looked at his daughter with a wary and searching glance.

She appeared not to hear him, but sat with her arms crossed, looking straight before her, and the unapproachable expression with which she always turned aside any attempt of her father's to couple the curate's name with hers.

The Provst knitted his bushy eyebrows. He could not make anything of his child. With a gloomy mien he continued his walk up and down in silence, and shortly after left the room.

Chapter Three

The curate had gone up to his own room, a spacious attic, quiet and secluded, surrounded by large lofts, a little world in itself. In spite of the sloping ceiling and scanty light from the one window, it was a comfortable room. There was a writing table, a sofa, and an old-fashioned mahogany desk; shelves filled with books, a big armchair, little mats on the floor, and a bed behind a screen. The air was fresh and flower-scented. The curate was one of those marvels among theologians — a non-smoker. He was also an ardent lover of flowers; the window was full of plants, and an ivy twined its pale green shoots round the window frame.

A small collection of family likenesses hung over the sofa between two big portraits of Luther and Melancthon. There was his father, a tall, thin, stately-looking man leaning against a table with his hat in his hand, and the broad ribbon of an order in the buttonhole of his tight-fitting coat. By his side hung a little Daguerreotype picture of his mother, surrounded by a wreath of yellow everlastings. It evidently dated from Mrs Hansted's maiden days. It was so bleached by the sun, that one could only through a haze catch a glimpse of a youthful face with the hair dressed high, and large, bright, wide open eyes. Besides these, there were portraits of the curate's brother, a lieutenant in the guards, — a handsome young man with a spirited and lively face; also of his sister, the wife of a consul-general, a little bird-like creature, hardly more than a child, with nervous twitching eyes and a sickly smile.

And here, by the writing table, sat Emanuel, the eldest of Councillor Hansted's children. He was sitting resting his chin on his hand, in a brown dressing gown, in the act of opening a letter. It was from his father; he had received it the previous day, but had put off reading it, so as not to be disturbed in the composition of his sermon. Now he opened it almost unwillingly, and read it through, at first hastily and abstractedly. There were the usual insignificant details of family events — his brother had been to a court ball, — the consul's birthday dinner, — his sister's baby had got a tooth, and so on. By degrees his attention was arrested. He read more slowly, word by word, sometimes with a thoughtful smile, and at last with a touch of sadness. The end ran thus:

"As you may imagine, my dear son, we are all delighted to hear that you are well and contented in your wilderness — as your brother in joke always speaks of it. There is no doubt that you have chosen a noble and exalted profession; and though I don't deny that I would rather have seen you choose a position in life more in accordance with our family traditions, and one which would not have taken you so far away from us; still, I can say with a clear conscience, that I and all of us wish you success and every blessing in the responsible work you have chosen. It is naturally rather difficult for us, who have always lived entirely in the society of our own cultivated class, to grasp thoroughly the possibility of any close or profitable companionship between people of such different circumstances and education; as, for example, you and the people among whom you have chosen to live. I do not deny that satisfactory intellectual intercourse — of course outside strictly religious ground — has always been to me an unsolved riddle. Perhaps this lies in my ignorance of the real conditions, and I only repeat that our best wishes follow you in your work."

Emanuel read this last part twice slowly through — and during the reading a darkening shadow spread over his face. Then the hand with the letter sank slowly on to his knee, and he remained motionless in this position, with his eyes fixed on the floor.

Suddenly he started up, and began striding up and down the room. He could not — he would not believe that his father and the others were right — that all his bright dreams were mere chimeras! — and yet, and yet! was it not this same gnawing doubt which tormented him now? Had he not in his innermost heart begun to lose faith, in at any rate possessing the powers to succeed in this vocation? He knew that he had tried with all his strength and will to perfect himself for his office. The closely written sheets in the drawer of his writing-table could witness to the untiring diligence, the conscientious care with which week after week he had prepared his sermons — hoping that in the end he might succeed in captivating his hearers with the power of his words and the strength of his faith. But in vain! — No sooner did he on Sunday go into the pulpit and see all the strange eyes turned upon him, than all the warmth and conviction of his words froze on his lips. In despair he heard his sentences ring hollow and empty under the echoing arches, while he noticed an ever-heavier drowsiness creeping over the whole congregation. It was as if an ever deeper and deeper gulf opened between him and the people, across which his voice could not reach — a dark and icy crevasse into which all his heavenward struggling words fell one by one like frozen birds. He stopped his troubled walk and stood in the deep embrasure of the window, looking out for a long time without moving. The sun shone with a golden light on the tall, fair-haired man, and as he stood there in his loose dressing gown, with his shoulder leaning against the edge of the wall, framed in, as it were, by the green ivy, he recalled the figure of some youthful monk gazing dreamily from his lonely cell, on the world which held all his longings. He could see almost the whole parish from his window. Straight below there was a corner of the Parsonage garden, and beyond this were a couple of the big Veilby plastered farms and the walled-in pond. Then he could follow the wide highway for a couple of miles, winding over the sloping fields, till, far away in the south, it dropped down between the three big, bare earth mounds behind which Skibberup hid itself so cosily that not a chimney pot was to be seen above the crests of the hills. Farther off, there was a glimpse of the lonely church, and along the whole of the eastern horizon the blue shallows of the fiord appeared, and the green and white shores of the opposite coast.

Emanuel had stood here every day, gazing out, and he already knew every house, tree and hill in the landscape. His eyes had dreamily followed — now the peasants, as with their ploughing teams they wandered one day in sleet and another in sunshine over the wet fields; now the boats of the Fiord fishermen cruising between the coasts, with their white or brown sails; now the hurrying vehicles of Skibberup as they rolled home from the town along the winding highroad, becoming smaller and smaller before his eyes at every turn, until like little mice they crept behind the three mole-hills in the distance. In the evening, when the last gleams of the sun had disappeared in the south-west, he saw the lights appearing one by one in the cottages, like stars in the sky.

Then in his loneliness he had put himself in imagination into the easily contented and toilsome life of the poor; and he thought of the time when, in his hatred of the society to which he belonged by birth, he had fancied himself related to these free children of the soil, and dreamt that he could live in frank intercourse with them as a friend and brother.

He now understood that he had made a mistake. His eyes were opened to the deep impassable gulf, which divided him from these children of the soil, who lived here in their half underground dwellings, digging, and busying themselves with the dark earth — gnomes — whose very being was a riddle, whose language was hardly intelligible, whose thoughts, words, dreams, sorrows and hopes were known to none.

And would it ever be otherwise? Was it not as if mankind had forgotten the magic word which could raise the hills on pillars of fire and bring the earth-folk to the light of day?

He was roused from his reflections by a lively chirping above his head.

He looked up. A Starling!

That was curious, he thought — he had been so taken up all day by his thoughts, that he had not noticed how the sun at last had burst through the cold fogs which had enveloped the land for weeks.

He looked about — and again a starling twittered near him — and then another and another — the whole garden seemed filled with the spring!

He smiled sadly. He thought how many times in the course of the winter he had longed for the coming of spring — because he had had a strange belief, that with it all would come right; that with the vernal break-up of the frost-bound fields and fiords, the spring of love which was rising in his heart would also be set free.

He turned towards the room, went to the writing-table and carefully put away his father's letter in one of the drawers, passed both his hands over his forehead and up through his hair, as if to drive away the heavy thoughts; changed his clothes, and taking his hat and umbrella, which stood by the door, left the room.

Chapter Four

He went down the creaking attic stairs, through the hall, and out of a gate at the side to reach the open fields through the garden.

Hardly had he passed the first big lawn, however, before he heard some one calling him. It was Miss Ragnhild's voice.

He was rather vexed. He would rather have been alone at this moment, and it was with a somewhat annoyed expression that he turned and went back.

Miss Ragnhild came towards him from the verandah — still wearing the flowered morning gown with the long tight bodice. As she stepped down the verandah stairs, a pair of pointed patent leather shoes were visible below the edge of her dress. She had a pale blue shawl over her shoulders, loosely knotted at the breast; and perched on her reddish waving hair was an immense straw hat, turned up at the back with an agrafe.

"Can I just speak to you before you go, Mr Hansted?" she asked with somewhat forced gaiety, looking at him closely with twitching eyes. "Do you mind going with me to the chestnut avenue, I want to see if I can find some violets."

They went through the garden together. This, which, as well as the house, was an inheritance of the "Millionaire parson," with the many lawns, shrubberies, big stone vases, its long alleys, and artificially clipped privet hedges, was more like a nobleman's seat than a homely Parsonage — and Provst Tönnesen took a pride in keeping it up in its former grandeur as far as he was able. Over a wide ditch, which divided the garden at one end, was built a wooden bridge in the Chinese style, with dragon's heads and a bamboo roof, — and over this bridge Miss Ragnhild and Emanuel now walked.

"Well," said the latter after some minutes silence, "may I ask what it is you wish to say to me?"

She laughed a little.

"Are you so inquisitive?"

"Yes, indeed," he answered, with an attempt to imitate her gay tone. "Besides which I am in a hurry!" As you see, I am dressed for a journey, for a pilgrimage. I am on the way to my Promised Land!"

"Your Promised Land? what do you mean?"

"Oh, I don't suppose I mean anything," he said, suddenly becoming grave again and looking down.

They walked on again a few minutes in silence.

She glanced at him a few times with her observant eyes. He walked by her side in his long coat, with both hands and his umbrella on his back, a little bent, and dragging slightly in his gait.

"What an ungrateful person you are!" she said, again trying to laugh. "I have half a mind to preach you an admonitory sermon. Haven't you noticed that both heaven and earth are smiling to you to-day, and that all the Lord's little birds are singing in emulation of each other above your head? And do you not see how I am extolling summer to-day! Or will nothing in the world bring a smile to your face now? I can tell you that I am on the high road to being a little offended with you. I am sure, for example, that you never noticed how I had decorated the luncheon table — entirely because you said one day that you thought much more of seeing a bunch of flowers on the table than a piece of beef. You know that, as far as I am concerned, a piece of beef is infinitely preferable."

He smiled half shyly. "I feel it thoroughly, Miss Ragnhild — I am a most unworthy person. Scold me as much as you like — I deserve it. But you will see, I shall improve. It's just a sort of childish complaint I am going through, I expect — a little old-fashioned romance perhaps. You know what the new-fashioned prophets preach. We all carry about an inheritance of moth-eaten, worn-out romance, they say — and either my father or my mother must have been endowed with an extra share of it."

"Your mother?"

"Yes — but let us talk about something else! You mustn't forget what you wanted to tell me. For I suppose it was not this?"

They had reached a broad avenue of chestnuts, which formed the boundary between the garden and the fields. A jubilant host of metallic shining starlings fluttered about in the sunshine among the tree-tops; and a warm balmy breeze brought in a scent of earth and fresh verdure from the fields. Between two trunks stood a rustic seat, before which Miss Ragnhild stopped, and said "Shall we sit down for a little while? The sun is so warm here."

She flicked away some dry leaves from the wooden seat with the tassels of her shawl, and sat down in one corner. Emanuel remained standing before her, leaning on his umbrella, and made no sign of sitting down.

She sat a moment bending forward with her hands folded in her lap, looking at the toes of her shoes. Then she said without lifting her head —

"You spoke of your mother — it has just occurred to me — have I dreamt it, or did you once tell me, that you were very young when your mother died."

"I?" said he, starting and looking down at her suddenly with an attentive glance. "Oh, I was fifteen or sixteen years old - but why do you ask about it?"

"Oh, I don't know..."

"Have you been talking to any one lately about my mother?"

"Yes, to-day father and I were talking about I think father once met someone who knew your mother."

The curate's eye darkened.

"Then I suppose your father also talked of — of my mother's end?"

"Yes."

A pained expression came over his face. After a moment's silence he said softly and with difficulty —

"My poor mother was a sacrifice to her time, to her family, and to the society to which you and I also belong, Miss Ragnhild; and which from our birth weaves such a web around us all, as slowly to take the life of those who have not courage or strength to break it asunder."

She looked up at him with astonishment, and said —

42

"What do you mean exactly?"

"Oh, I mean that if we were candid, we should be obliged to acknowledge that we all drag about a more or less heavy burden of loathing of life, world weariness, lonesomeness, or whatever we like to call the modern disease which is the bitter fruit of our over-culture. There are some who are strong enough to bear this burden without being entirely crippled; but it is not therefore always the most insignificant or the weakest whose hearts break. You will see, we may perhaps all sink down in the battle — especially we poor caricatures of humanity, who are begotten in the feverish life of the towns, born among chimney pots, telegraph wires, railways and trams — how many generations do you think we shall last? — And that is just the desperate part," he continued, with a changed voice, as he fell back into his old tormenting thoughts. "Can't you see, Miss Ragnhild, how topsy turvey it is that it should be my office to teach others to live and die — I, who need to learn to live my own life rightly — and just of those very people whom I am set to teach? Or is it not true that we ought to envy, with all our hearts, the poor labourer who toils week in week out; happily, and without complaint, eats his dry bread and sleeps soundly on old straw? Is greater wisdom of life to be found? But what folly it is that I, a poor corrupt, monstrous product of culture, should be a teacher of the sound — an example to the undefiled! I assure you, Miss Ragnhild, I never cross the threshold of the most miserable hovel without my heart beating with holy reverence. I feel that I ought to take off my shoes — that I am entering a sacred place where human passions are still preserved in all their pristine beauty and nobility, just as the Almighty instilled them into mankind in the morning of life."

He had entered upon his usual passionate praise of the life of the countryman, about which he and Miss Ragnhild had had many a warm debate in the course of the winter. Miss Ragnhild confessed openly that she hated country life — according to her opinion it was a living burial; nor did she conceal that she looked upon peasants as beings who belonged to a lower level — a sort of now creeping, now usurping, but always evil-smelling semi-human creatures, with whom she desired to come as little as possible in contact.

On this occasion also she combated Emanuel's views most strenuously. She leant back against the seat and looked at him with an unconstrained smile.

"If many of these peasants," she said, "are content with their dirt and mouldy straw, and hardly even wish for anything better, it only shows how little in reality they are removed from dumb brutes, swine, for example, in whom all the feelings of the heart are undoubtedly preserved in unadulterated swinishness."

"But it is no use for us to talk about it," she concluded, gaily, "you have once for all been irremediably bitten by some crazy digger of ditches, and it is folly on my part to try and convince you. This illusion will turn to stern reality one of these days. Only wait!"

She laughed — and as she sat there in her bright, distinguished-looking costume, self-controlled in every line of her slim figure, from the tip of her little patent leather shoe to the gigantic fancy straw hat, which threw shadows like a lace veil over the upper part of her pale face with the ruddy lips — one might very well doubt that she belonged to the same race of humanity as the heavy grey creatures clad in homespun, toilers of the earth, among whom she was condemned to live.

Emanuel, who felt hurt by her words, made a sign as if to go. Before doing so he turned towards her once again and said:

"I should like to know what it was you wished to say to me — you are forgetting that you have not told me yet."

Miss Ragnhild coloured slightly. She had had no other reason for calling him than that she wished to talk to him, to try and cheer him a little.

Then she hit upon saying:

"Well you see, Mr Hansted — as you perhaps know, we are going to have a little festivity to-day at the Parsonage."

"Yes, I think I have heard a little bird whisper it."

"Oh well, make fun if you like. A thing of that sort is always an event in the country, where nothing more interesting happens from year's end to year's end — which for the rest only proves what I said before on the subject. But enough of that. — As I daresay you can imagine, I shall be a most charming hostess to my guests. They are, as far as I know, Messrs Peter Niels, Niels Petersen, Peter Nielsen Petersen, and Niels Petersen Nielsen. — Oh, you needn't knit your brows in such a scandalized fashion, I have not the slightest objection to these good people. Only, I cannot reconcile myself to their spitting on my good carpets — yes, last time one of them did so. Possibly that kind of thing is a manifestation of the spontaneity of feeling of which you spoke before so finely, but I would none the less rather be without it. — Now I wanted to ask you, Mr Hansted, to be as amiable as possible to our guests this evening. And if anything should happen to me; one of my bad headaches, for instance — you will be so good as to be my gallant representative among the ladies."

"You can, as you know — command me," answered Emanuel, as he lifted his hat and bowed with ironical politeness. "Is there any other way in which I can serve you, Miss Ragnhild?"

"Yes, I daresay you will be accommodating enough not to be too unpunctual for once. I believe my father would be very impatient on this occasion if we had to wait for you. Rather come half an hour too soon, then you can help me with some of the arrangements into the bargain."

"I will do my best, but then you must allow me to leave you now. Besides, I see your father coming along in a hurry. You may be sure that there is something wrong with the salads. I have the honour to take leave of you."

Provst Tönnesen had indeed made his appearance at the end of the garden, walking with his hands behind him — he was evidently preparing a speech. But no sooner did he catch sight of the young pair by the seat, than he hurriedly turned and continued his walk in the opposite direction through the garden.

Chapter Five

Miss Ragnhild remained sitting a little while longer on the seat with her hands on her lap, looking thoughtfully before her. Then she rose and walked slowly towards the Parsonage. She was met by the old servant who was upset by the bustle of the day, and who had been quite unhappy at her long absence; she had a string of questions as to the preparation of the food and the setting out of the festive table. Miss Ragnhild gave her directions in a short, decided tone, and then went into the sitting room, where she sat down at the window, with a book, an English novel which she took hap-hazard out of the bookcase.

After reading for a quarter of an hour, she looked at the clock in the corner. It was three o'clock. She laid down her book, got up, and busied herself about the room, stood a moment looking at the parrot, which had gone to sleep in its cage, and at last sat down at the grand piano, where she began to play one of Chopin's preludes.

Again she looked at the clock. Ten minutes past three.

Then she once more struck a few chords, but broke off suddenly, rose and took up a newspaper from the heavy, round mahogany table in the middle of the room, and sat down by the window again. She remained sitting, with the paper unfolded on her knee, her chin resting in her slender, white hand, her glance wandering slowly over the big empty courtyard, and the thatched roofs of the stables — until the clock at last struck half past three. Then she rose and went into her room to dress.

The visitors were expected at six o'clock, and as the ordinary dinner was to be passed over on account of the party, there was plenty of time for a careful toilet.

Even under ordinary circumstances, changing her dress was one of the chief events of the day to Miss Ragnhild. She regularly passed the two hours before dinner in her almost over-luxuriously furnished bedroom, in which there was always a delicate odour of the essence of violets.

It was one of her amusements to stand before her long glass, looking at herself as she dressed and undressed; she would admire her neck, her shoulders, her loosened hair, try a new way of doing it, or a new combination of colours for her costumes — all this not out of empty vanity, or love of display — who could she care to dazzle here? — but because it gave transient satisfaction to her longing for beauty, delicacy, and harmony.

Besides, what else was there for her to do? — She worked at her music every morning — and this was her happiest time. But the doctor had strictly forbidden her to spend more than three hours a day at the piano. She spent

45

two hours in reading — preferably foreign languages — and at need she could kill two hours in household duties, although her personal help was quite superfluous. There remained eight long weary hours — what was she to do with them? Walk? but in the eight winter months the fields and roads were impassible morasses, or the snow lay round the Parsonage like an insurmountable wall. Even in the summer, the sight of the broad silent fields, the bare monotonous stone dykes, the everlasting grey or blue fiord, had a most depressing effect upon her. All this lifeless wilderness by which she was surrounded filled her with horror. And the living objects were worse than the inanimate. Worst of all, was to walk through the village, where she knew beforehand what people she would meet, in what places, and at what occupation; where she was obliged to return the obtrusive greetings of the peasants, and to answer the rambling speeches of the half-clad labourer's wives about the weather, harvest prospects, and night frosts. She therefore generally restricted her walks to a solitary path leading from the Parsonage to the sand banks. She would take a little brisk exercise here towards sundown — until the sound of a party of returning field-labourers, or the suffocating odour of a newly-manured field drove her home again.

She had lived in this solitude for eight years. She was born in a provincial town of Jutland, where her father was assistant schoolmaster. From her thirteenth year, when she lost her mother, till her confirmation, she stayed in Copenhagen with some aunts, to complete her education in a superior girl's school.

She only took up her permanent abode at the end of her sixteenth year.

She had come with her young heart swelling with bright hopes. She had learnt from her novels, and the theatres, that the flower of Danish womanhood was to be found in the daughters of the country Parsonages, whose charms had been sung by the poets, and whose possession all noble-minded young men desired. Nor was she entirely unconscious of her own advantages — her white skin and rippling auburn hair had already, as a schoolgirl, attracted attention in her native town in Jutland, so she went about every day in silent, sweet expectation, prepared to receive the homage which was her due.

She still remembered plainly, how in those days she wandered about the garden with her hair in a thick plait, hanging down her back, light kid mittens, and a fresh moss rose in her bosom.

At one time she would sit dreaming in the shade of a softly sighing tree, at another she would climb the dyke by the field, and shading her eyes with her hands, would look out into the sunlit landscape — as if every day she really expected two wandering "Students" to appear on the horizon. [1] She pictured to herself exactly what they looked like, how — dusty and sunburnt — they would peep inquisitively in at the garden gate, and how her father would appear on the verandah and ask them in; how at first they would be shy, but gradually become lively and frank, and would end by singing Bellman's Songs [2] in the garden by moonlight; how at last one of them, — not

46

the merry and amusing one, but the one with the deep dark eyes — would, on taking leave, press her hand and stammer some agitated words about not forgetting him, and how in the following year he would come back, having taken his degree, and ask her father for her hand with earnest words.

But no tourists ever came to that desolate corner of the country, and summer after summer went by without the smallest sign of a romantic episode. Ragnhild Tönnesen used to smile when she looked back at her youthful dreams. She had often been troubled later by suitors among the beer-fattened Squire's sons, who evidently were quite unable to grasp that she — especially now that she was no longer in her first youth — did not gratefully accept their offers. But otherwise the years she had passed at her father's side had slipped by without any experiences of interest whatever. Now and then, when she looked back at her life, she could hardly believe that she was not more than four and twenty, and still in the height of her bloom. She felt certain that she must have begun to grow old. In short, there was nothing in the world which realized her anticipations except her music. Even her annual visit to Copenhagen, which in the first few years of her country life had been like one long fete lasting three weeks, and for which she had prepared herself for months with delight, no longer gave her any real pleasure. After a time she had become strange to city life, her old friends and acquaintances were scattered, her aunts were dead — and then after it, her home life seemed doubly empty, and nature around her doubly dismal in its mute stony lifelessness.

Therefore it was not at all agreeable to her when her father decided to take a curate. She did not want to be disturbed in the state of somnolency into which, by degrees, she had dropped. When, in addition, she perceived that people, even before the arrival of the curate, coupled their names, it did not dispose her more pleasantly towards him: on this account the relations between them were at first decidedly cool, not to say strained. But when she gradually saw that the new house-mate only wanted to live in the same undisturbed reserve as she herself, she became more easily reconciled to his daily presence. When, at the same time, she discovered his taste for music, and that he had made the acquaintance of some of the most renowned composers at his father's house, about whom it amused her to hear, he began little by little to rouse her interest. As Emanuel also felt an even greater need for someone to talk to, and in whom to confide, an unconstrained and half confidential relation arose between them little by little, and almost without their knowing it, which roused the Provst's attention and reflection.

When, however, the Provst — and others — laid plans for the future of the young people founded on this relationship, they rested on a complete misunderstanding. Although Miss Ragnhild was in reality the younger of the two, she considered herself the superior of the curate, both in age and experience. She looked upon him as a right-minded and warm-hearted, but slightly peculiar person, who had been driven by unfortunate circumstances at home to seek new worlds among strangers. Even his name, Emanuel, had from the first thrown a comic air over his personality. His youth and helplessness had later awakened her motherly instincts, and the more depressed and reserved he became in the course of the winter, the more she had seen him suffer under the disappointments she knew so well herself, so much the more she felt the necessity of winning his confidence, so as if possible to cheer and distract him a little.

From the very beginning there had not been the slightest trace of love on either side — and in this respect there was no misunderstanding between them either.

[1] This refers to one of Johan Ludwig Heiberg's (1791 1860) Vaudevilles, "The adventures of a walking tour," always much played in Denmark, in which the heroes are two students.
[2] Charles Michael Bellman's (1741-1795) "Swedish Student Songs,"

Chapter Six

Emanuel went out by a gate at the further end of the garden leading into the open fields. Here he found himself on the highest point of the district, the so-called "Parsonage Hill," from the top of which a wide view was gained. On every side were pale green fields of rye, which glistened in the sun among the dark ploughed land; light blue mists lay over the fens and swampy places, ditches and ponds steamed, and the whole land was enveloped in fruitful vapours, the fresh spring air was filled with sunlight, and the song of birds, all heralding the festal entrance of summer any day. Emanuel took a path which led from the Parsonage, through a number of outlying fields towards the fiord. It was the same path taken by Miss Ragnhild in her hurried little sunset promenades. He did not think of this however, nor was it because of this that it had become his favourite walk. If they were both attached to it, the reason was the same for him as well as for her; they could have the most solitude here. In their loneliness they involuntarily sought still lonelier spots, and in these remote fields only an occasional cottage was to be seen or a solitary peasant ploughing.

In the course of the winter, Emanuel had wandered here every day in his long coat, and with his inseparable companion, the black silk umbrella, which was as dear to him as a trusted friend. He had often roamed about for half a day among the hills and along the deserted shore without rhyme or reason; and in this intimate communion with nature he at last found some recompense for the loss of human intercourse. Everything here continued to be fresh and wonderful to him. He had never before imagined that anything could be so captivating, as, for example, the slow passage of grey wintry clouds over the earth; or anything so enchanting as listening to the wild cries of the crows as they flew homewards over the fields at sunset.

His heart leapt with delight when, one day in the beginning of February, he discovered the first pale shoots in the ditches — and the first lark! Never would he forget the moment when, in the deep silence of the fields, he suddenly heard the ethereal trills of a lark, sure forerunner of the summer, while all around, still lay bound in winter's grasp.

On this occasion he went down to the shore, where he was in the habit of spending some time watching the gulls as they flew about, mute and restless, as if guarding some great secret. But to-day the beach was empty. The warmth and the exhalations of the meadows had driven the flocks of birds towards the mouth of the fiord and the sea. He continued his walk along the shore, revelling in the sight of the vast blue shallows of the fiord, in which the distant fishing villages and the wooded slopes of the opposite shore were reflected with wonderful clearness. At last he climbed a hill to the south, whence he again had a wide view of the country. Skibberup lay straight below him with its three bare earth mounds.

He always felt specially attracted by the sight of this village, which, with its clusters of small cottages, its spreading pond, and its many windings and turnings, seemed to him much more idyllic than Veilby, with its brand-new, formal peasant farms which he had before him daily. He was also doubly saddened when he reflected that it was in this very village that the anti-clerical movement had its head-quarters; and when his eye suddenly fell on a low, dilapidated building in the middle of the village, over the thatched roof of which a "Dannebrog's" [1] flag waved, a pang shot through his heart. He guessed that it was the "Meeting House" from which Hansen the weaver carried on his angry battle against the church.

At one end of the village, lying by itself, was a little place with yellow washed outbuildings, which Emanuel at once recognised as the farm to which he had been fetched in the sledge on that winter evening to administer the Holy Communion to the owner's suffering daughter. He had often thought since of that evening and the strangers among whom he had come in such a strange way to inaugurate his priestly work. He had often been inclined to renew his visit to them and to ask after their daughter; but hitherto he had no more summoned up courage to do so than to mix with any of the other people of the district. His innate shyness soon caused him to draw back from all personal intimacies, when — almost immediately after his first sermon — the people showed their unfriendly feeling towards him so plainly.

But to-day it seemed as if the sun and the spring air endued him with fresh courage, and he resolved seriously to pay his visit. He said to himself that he could not go on living here in this way, that a decision must be come to. He felt at this moment with renewed strength, that he owed it to himself, no longer to put off defining his position, but he must make a decisive effort to discover the reason of the ill-feeling which had arisen so suddenly against him.

He buttoned his coat, dusted it, and drew on his gloves, and walked down with firm steps towards the village.

[1] The Danish Flag which fell from heaven at the prayer of Andreas Suneson, Archbishop of Lund, when he led the Christian army of Valdemar Second against the heathen Esthonians in 1219.

Chapter Seven

It was the first time that Emanuel had been seen in Skibberup without his official gown and ruff. His appearance, therefore, aroused considerable attention all over the village. The spring air and the day of rest had tempted people out of their houses everywhere; even the old cripples had hobbled out from the chimney corners, and sat on the doorsteps, sunning themselves. Both men and women were busy digging in the cottage gardens, and bareheaded children ran about playing. Few, either of men or women, had a greeting for the young priest, though they all looked up from their work, and followed him with their eyes as far as they could. Some of the youths who were leaning over the fences by the girls, or standing in the gateways smoking long pipes, were beguiled by the bright sunshine into insolent smiles and half-audible remarks as he passed.

In the doorway of a low house stood a man in blue striped shirt-sleeves, with a child in his arms. It was the big black-bearded snow-clearer who had made the hearty little speech of welcome to Emanuel on the evening that he went to the sick girl. Now the man only smiled, showing his white teeth when Emanuel passed; and the child in his arms beginning to cry, he said, quite loud, as he wiped its nose with his fingers, "There's naught to be frightened of, my lass! it's on'y his rev'rence, our young parson!"

Although Emanuel was already tolerably accustomed to the incivility of the people, and although he had brought himself to believe that the reason of the discord between himself and the congregation was principally owing to a want in himself, he was often obliged to struggle against the dull wrath which was roused in him, more especially by the conduct of the young people. To-day, too, he found it difficult to preserve his equanimity, and he did not breathe freely till he reached Anders Jörgen's little farm in the southern end of the village. It was not without emotion that he passed under the low gateway and recognised the lantern which still twisted slowly round at the end of the cord, under the rafters. In the yard he stopped and looked around him. Not a creature was to be seen or heard. He went up to the low dwelling-house, entered the passage, and knocked twice at a door to the left. No one answered.

After a moment's hesitation he opened the door and went into the broad, low-ceilinged living room, with its equipment of antique furniture, which had attracted his attention on yonder evening. The room was empty. Nor was any sound to be heard in the adjoining rooms except the loud ticking of the tall old clock in the side room where the girl had lain ill. He was at his wit's end. He knocked at various doors leading to different parts of the house, but he received no answer anywhere. The house appeared to be deserted. He remained standing a moment in the middle of the floor, lost in thought, while his eye wandered over the room. He recognised the heavy oak table and the benches under the small, many-paned

HANSINE·
AT· HOME·

51

windows, the large square stove, the dark earthen floor strewn with sand, the spinning wheel, and the blue striped curtains of the alcove bed in one corner of the room. A row of shining pewter plates stood upon a high shelf, and upon the wall behind the old armchair by the stove, by way of ornament, hung a cross of straw, a bunch of sweet herbs, and two framed samplers, bearing the date of 1798. All bore witness to a sense of order and scrupulous cleanliness. An air of simple, festive, Sunday comfort rested over the little sunny peasant's home, with which Emanuel was charmed. He involuntarily compared this simplicity with the gorgeous luxury of his own home, furnished with all the modern townspeople's outfit of thick carpets, velvet upholstery, heavy *portières* and exotic plants, in which the depraved taste of advanced civilization indulged. On the wall between the windows he discovered a small collection of portraits of well-known men in simple wood-cuts. There were Tscherning, [1] Grundtvig, Monrad, [2] and a few others whom he knew. The centre place was occupied by a larger picture which showed Frederick VII. signing the constitution. Emanuel remembered the same picture in his mother's room - and it moved him strangely to meet it again after so many years in these surroundings.

He was roused from his observations by hearing steps in the courtyard. From a little gate between the stables came a young girl with a yoke on her shoulders, and milk pails suspended, followed by the same white-haired lad who had driven the sledge on that winter night. The young girl had on her Sunday best, a cherry-coloured dress fancifully braided over the bosom and on the sleeves. She had fastened up the skirt in her belt in front, and had a light handkerchief tied round her head, which gave her round-cheeked face a still rounder and rosier effect. A white-footed cat was arching its back, and purring round the milk pails, its attention being divided between the young girl and two little kittens carried by the boy. About the middle of the yard it bounded towards a hollow stone in front of an empty dog kennel, where it was evidently used to having its ration of milk given to it. But as the girl walked dreamily on as if she had forgotten it to-day, the animal sprang towards her and clawed the edge of her skirt. Then she smiled half-seriously, turned and poured a liberal allowance of the still steaming milk into the hollow stone. But now the cat's martyrdom began; instead of putting down the kittens, the boy lifted them above his head, defending himself meanwhile with his foot, against the raging mother which tried to climb up his leg, and then turned to the girl with a woeful expression as if accustomed to look there for protection. The girl pleaded for the poor animal, though she was not able to help smiling a little, but the boy would not give up his prize, and continued to dance about the yard, the cat at his heels.

Emanuel stood at the window silently surveying this scene. His glance rested especially on the young girl, whom he easily recognised as the daughter of the house. He had imagined her to be taller and handsomer; but to make up for this, her trim, little, neatly built figure disclosed peculiar earnestness of purpose coupled with such youthful bloom, that he had difficulty in taking his eyes off her.

As the boy continued his game, he thought it time to make his presence known. He went back to the door by which he had entered, and stepped out on to the stone flags in front of the entrance.

Brother and sister both uttered a little startled cry when they caught sight of him. With a burning blush the young girl hurriedly pulled her skirt down and tore off the handkerchief she had worn for milking, while her brother hastily let go the kittens, and disappeared through the nearest barn door.

Emanuel went down the steps and along to greet her.

"Pray, don't let me disturb you," he said, lifting his brown plush hat a couple of inches from his head. "I happened to be passing, and looked in to ask after you. I see you have quite recovered since last I saw you."

"Thank you," she muttered, looking behind her with a dark, uneasy glance, as if for succour.

At this moment a stable door opened, and old Anders Jörgen came tramping out in heavy metal tipped wooden shoes, with a halter in his hand. He was in a black and white flannel shirt, and a fur cap with a tassel covered his wiry grey hair. He was humming a merry tune, but no sooner did his half-blind eyes make out Emanuel than he also became rigid with astonishment, and threw away the halter as if he had been caught in a crime.

Emanuel went towards him, holding out his hand in a friendly manner. The old man could not get over his flurry, but went on stammering out confused excuses for his "work-a-day look."

"Oh, never mind about that! The proverb says, 'A workman is not ashamed of his tools,'" said Emanuel, becoming more easy at the sight of their embarrassment.

"I hope you are well, Anders Jörgen? It is a long time since I saw you."

"Thank ye — thank ye; it's just this way, ye see, the beasts mun be looked after, be it work-a-day or holy day." The old man went on excusing himself. "We've just got two new-calved cows — an one o' them's got a chill — an ye can't very weel neglect her."

"Of course not — don't reproach yourself!" said Emanuel, smiling. "I was just passing and thought I should like to see how time goes with you. I see that your daughter — isn't her name Hansine?"

"Ay, your reverence."

"I see she has quite recovered. I hope she has got over her illness entirely."

"I'm much obliged to ye, sir. I think she's quite hearty again, thank the Lord; but, if you please, won't your rev'rence step inside? Mother'll be here directly, she's only slipped out to see a woman at the Plantation."

They walked over the yard together, and went into the room where the sun still shone brightly into the windows, throwing little squares of golden light over the table and the sanded floor. Anders Jörgen offered Emanuel the seat of honour in the old arm-chair by the stove, while he himself, in white stocking feet, sat on the corner of a wooden chair by the alcove. He folded his

53

hands solemnly on his knees, palms upwards, as he did during the sermon at church, and remained sitting in this position, listening to every sound outside with an uneasy expression, in the plainly visible hope that it was his wife returning to set him free from his misery.

Emanuel, on the contrary, felt more and more at his ease in the comfortable little peasant's room. He quickly found a subject for conversation in the fine spring weather, and with a degree of ease which astonished himself, he talked of the joy and gratitude which the farmers in particular ought to feel at seeing how the Almighty was blessing their labours. He did not pay any attention to Anders Jörgen's restless abstraction. On the other hand, he often looked in the course of the conversation with attention towards the daughter of the house. She had come into the room, and sat down with a piece of work by the window, where the sun fell on to her erect little figure, and threw a warm glow over her dark brown plaits. She had completed her toilet by a broad crotchet collar which fell over her shoulders in points; she had smoothed her hair with water, and fastened it up in coils. She made her entrance with a somewhat stiff upright bearing, and a rather defiant expression, as if trying to indemnify herself for the state of confusion in which the curate had found her. But from the moment that she seated herself on the bench at the furthest end of the room from Emanuel, she remained immovably bent over her work, half turned away, as if she was trying as much as possible to efface herself; while, in reality, her position and the colour of her cheeks plainly betrayed that she was all ears in her distant corner, and was eagerly drinking in every word of the curate's.

It did not occur to Emanuel that his glance sometimes rested in a rather free and direct way upon her. He was so delighted at having at last found a small circle of listeners, that by degrees he forgot all his shyness. All at once, steps were heard on the flags in the yard. Anders Jörgen moved in his chair with a sigh of relief, and the young girl along by the window threw a hasty glance through the panes to prepare the newcomer. But she suddenly changed colour, and with a startled, almost frightened glance, her eyes sought her father's.

A moment later three discreet raps sounded on the door.

[1] Minister of War in 1848.
[2] Cultus-Minister in the famous "March Ministry" of 1848, which drafted the Constitution. Afterwards Bishop of Laaland and Falster. The *"Bishop"* of the story.

Chapter Eight

The new arrival was the tall, thin, and somewhat bent man, with the curious cat-like face, who had been the object of so much attention among Emanuel's audience in the morning. He remained standing a moment by the door, looking about him and smiling with his crooked, drawn-up mouth. Then he said "Good-day" in a drawling voice, and went round shaking hands.

Old Anders Jörgen, who rose from his chair immediately, became quite pale with consternation, and looked at the stranger with a bewildered, imploring glance, which the latter evidently tried to avoid. The whole bearing of the stranger made an unusually unpleasant impression on Emanuel. He remembered having seen the same face in church occasionally, where it had also inspired him with extraordinary repulsion. This feeling was not lessened when the stranger turned towards him, and, fixing him with a glance which was partly hidden by his red, swollen eyelids, introduced himself in these words: "I am Hansen the weaver."

Emanuel had need of all his self-command not to lose his composure. He felt himself turning fiery red.

He just kept presence of mind enough to return the man's greeting with the right amount of cold reserve, after which he continued his conversation with Anders Jörgen. After a time, the weaver's presence even had the involuntary effect of adding a touch of high-bred clerical dignity to his bearing, with a fleeting resemblance to that of Provst Tönnesen.

In the meantime, it did not seem that the weaver had any evil intentions. He took a seat on the bench at the end of the table, and sat there leaning forward with his elbows on his knees, and both his big red hands over his mouth, as if he had only joined them as an attentive listener. But it was not long before his face began twitching and grimacing, while he first cleared his throat, then coughed in a forced manner, and looked about smilingly from the alcove to the window where Hansine sat with heightened colour and swelling bosom, stooping over her work and not daring to lift her eyes. Emanuel became paler and paler. The smothered anger which had come over him at the behaviour of the young men in the village, began to struggle forth in his bosom, and caused him to stammer. He still, however, kept the mastery over his wrath, but when the weaver began to mutter behind his hands, and to make half audible sarcastic remarks on his conversation, his patience gave way. With a mixture of youthful passion and clerical displeasure he turned towards him and exclaimed: "I do not know if it is your intention to drive me from the room, but I may tell you that you will not succeed, and that I will not put up with your interruptions."

Anders Jörgen rose from his seat by the alcove in consternation and wished to make peace, but Emanuel's blood was up, and it was not easy to stop him. "I know you very well by hearsay, weaver Hansen," he continued with quivering lips. "Provst Tönnesen has told me a good deal about you, and I tell you that you had better take care. Neither the Provst nor I intend to tolerate your attempt to sow discord or dissension among the congregation any longer. As to what concerns myself, I warn you that my patience has limits, and that I will not put up with your continued efforts to thwart me in my work. I know that I have struggled to the best of my ability to form friendly relations with the congregation, and I have tried to win both parties, to

55

smooth out their mutual difficulties. But if you are bent upon war — well, then, I am ready for you! We shall see who is the strongest!"

There was a dead silence in the room after his words. Even the weaver sat a moment holding his head as if he had had a blow. But soon the same distorted, irritating leer passed over his contracted countenance. It almost looked as if the young priest's anger was downright pleasing to him.

After a moment's silence he said in his slow imperturbable manner —

"You wrong me, sir, I'm sure. You say you know me; and know what a bad, reckless person I am, and that you have heard it from the Provst himself, so there must be reason in it. The Provst has so often condemned me to hell fire that I can't help thinkin' he's sincere. But you know very well, sir, that things don't always fall out exac'ly as the Provsts preach, and perhaps I'm not quite so black as the Provst would like to make me out. I won't deny, as far as that goes, that I came here to have a little talk with you, between four walls, as we say, for it has long been in my mind to pay you a visit. It seems to me that there might very well be a few things for us to talk about. When I heard that you had gone into Anders Jörgen's, it struck me it was best not to lose the chance."

"I am sure I do not see what we can have to talk about," exclaimed Emanuel shortly, in a voice still trembling with anger.

"Well, well, perhaps not," continued the weaver just as soberly, but in a changed tone, while the smile for a moment left his face, and he watched the curate narrowly as if to test him. "I believe all the same that you take us Skibberup folks in the wrong way. We always have our own way of taking things. We somehow speak plainly about everything, and because of that you're annoyed with me to-day, sir. All I can say is, that the last thing I should wish to do, would be to offend you."

"Well, then, I don't understand your behaviour," Emanuel answered in the same stand-off manner, although he was beginning to be calmer, and to be a little ashamed of his outburst.

"No, that's just it, sir! that's exac'ly what it is, you don't understand us. We've seen that all along, and we've been heartily sorry for it, I can tell you. And that's why we all thought it would be best to have a talk to you about it."

The sudden gravity with which he said these words, and the quiet self-confidence with which he spoke in the name of the congregation, made Emanuel hesitate. He looked at the weaver with an uncertain glance and said "If you really have anything to talk to me about, I am of course at your service, but it seems to me that the opportunity might have been better chosen."

"Look there now, isn't that just what I said, we Skibberup folk are just as awkward as a cat in getting through a chimney! All the same, sir, you'll allow me to tell you that it's not to be wondered at that we were a bit excited by having you here among us. You see, we never could leave off thinkin' of the woman who came to the Friends of the people in these parts, like the Holy Virgin herself; why, her memory lives now amongst us, as our purest an' best."

"I do not understand whom you mean," said Emanuel, looking at him in astonishment.

"Who I mean?" said the weaver, staring at him as if he could fix him in his chair by the power of his eye. "Well, who else should I mean than she, who of all people was nearest to you, Pastor Hansted, and who long since was freed from her sorrows and sufferings — your mother."

Emanuel started, had he heard aright?

"My mother?" he exclaimed in a low tone, and his eyes involuntarily sought the little collection of portraits on the wall between the windows.

"Well, it certainly was before she became your mother that she was to us Friends of the people what we never can forget, though we did have proofs that she didn't entirely throw us off when she became your father's wife. Now, I suppose you will understand, sir, what joy and pride arose among us when we heard that Mrs Hansted's son was coming to be our curate. We thought that must indeed be a minister after our own hearts. And we do need a man of that kind here; yes, we need him sorely, Pastor Hansted?"

Emanuel could not get over his astonishment at hearing his mother mentioned for the second time in the course of the day, and this time, too, as a never-to-be-forgotten protectress — the mother whose memory was already wiped out in his own home, and whose name was whispered there with bated breath, so as not to wake up recollections of the shame, which her unhappy end had thrown over the respected Hansted family.

"But see here now, you'll give me leave to tell you, sir," while he steadily watched the young priest. "You'll allow me to tell you honestly, Pastor Hansted, that we have not exac'ly found in you what we so much hoped to find, and I daresay you've perceived that yourself. Now there are your sermons, for example — don't be angry," he broke off with feigned anxiety, when at his last words he saw a cloud pass over the curate's face. "At any rate you won't mind my saying that, although we are glad you do not, as certain others do, speak to us as if we were a flock of dumb animals; and although we see that your sermons are carefully thought out, well expressed, poetical, and what you would call well delivered, still they are only the same as we have so often heard before. And what is it our good priests are always telling us peasants? It is that we are to be obedient and virtuous, neither to steal nor to swear, but to turn to the Lord in our sorrows, and trust in the grace of God, and so on. But we know all that by heart, and we shall not be better men even if we were to hear the whole catechism every Sunday in first rate poetry! No, if a man like you, Pastor Hansted, would tell us something about yourself, instead of about ourselves, because you can't tell us anything on that subject that we don't know better than you do; no, what we want is something really about yourself, and how you, with your reading and education have arrived at your views of Christianity and the life of the people, then we should learn something, and that's what we need, so as to see how other people live and think in their conditions of life. That's what we want our minister to help us to, you see. I don't know if you understand me, sir. I am only a working man,

57

and I have never studied either for orders or even to be parish clerk, so I'm not up to picking and choosing my words perhaps."

Emanuel let him have his talk out. He felt keenly how humiliating it was for him to be obliged to listen to this harangue, especially in the presence of others. But he was not able to force out a word to stop it, because in his heart of hearts he was obliged to confess that the weaver was right. Yes, that this man had put into words the very thoughts which had latterly been troubling him so much. Only when the weaver stopped, and he perceived how all eyes were fixed expectantly on him, did he pull himself together and answered —

"Perhaps I have not, as you may suppose, altogether grasped your meaning, and I am possibly not able to agree with you entirely in all your views. But I appreciate the frankness with which you have mentioned them to me. Such mutual frankness is certainly the first condition towards a closer understanding becoming possible between us."

"Yes, that's our idea too," said the weaver with sudden eagerness. "And that's just why we thought it would be a good plan to talk things over. So far, we only know you in church — nor will I deny that we've several times liked what we heard there — but we always think we would like to get nearer to you than that; we country folk are an inquisitive set, we like to get to know our ministers well, so that we may go to them freely with all our difficulties and whatever we have on our minds. We peasants who labour in the same round day in and day out — we badly need some one among us who can give us information and teaching about things you can't exactly speak of from the pulpit. But that's what our good priests never really understand, and that's why we're often on such bad terms.

"See here now, for example, we've a sort of Meeting House, as we call it, in Skibberup. I daresay you've heard about it, sir, and know what sort of a 'den of iniquity' it is; for that's what the Provst calls it. But for all that, we don't do anything but meet in a friendly way, and talk over whatever we like, or we read aloud various books, either religious ones, or the "Readings for the People," as we call them. We think it must be just as good a pastime listening to good words as to lie snoozing on the benches all the winter evenings, or to spend time in gambling, and other dissipations — the custom in the good old days that the Provst talks so much about. It's easy to see that what we peasant folk can have to talk to each other about, can't be much to the purpose; no, if we could get a man like you, Mr Hansted, to visit us and talk to us in a homely way, and tell us anything you like, it would be another matter; that would be something that would give us real pleasure and that we should thank you for. We all think, when all's said and done, that you're an honest, civil-spoken gentleman that we could get to like very much. Then you're as like your mother as two peas, especially in your expression, as far as I can remember, having only seen her once, many a year ago, at one of our friendly meetings at Sandinge. So I'll promise you there'd be joy on the day it became known that the curate would visit us in the Meeting House, because then we'd know that we'd found what we so long and earnestly had wished for. It

58

was only these few words I wanted to say to you, sir, and you mustn't be angry that I've made so free. I can assure you I've done it for the best."

Emanuel continued silent.

He was so curiously dazed by the weaver's words, which suddenly opened up to him a vista of the fulfilment of all the longings stored in his soul. He no longer knew what to believe. Was this man, about whom he had heard so much evil, really a friend? or was it all a cunning device to entrap him? And Anders Jörgen and his daughter? Were they secretly in league with him? He had accidentally caught the strained expectant expression with which the young girl along in the corner, at her work, watched him, as if by her glance she would steal the answer from his lips. Instead of answering he got up to go, he felt that he no longer had the mastery over his thoughts, and feared to lose his self-possession altogether before the strangers. With an apology that his time to-day did not permit him to continue the discussion, he took his hat and began to take leave. Amid a deep silence he went round shaking hands. When he left the room no one accompanied him.

Chapter Nine

Emanuel left the farm with hasty steps. To avoid passing through the village again he went by the nearest slopes back to the shore. He soon recovered himself in the fresh air. The stuffy air of the little peasant's room and sitting still so long had both contributed to the confusion which had overcome him.

He was in a curious state, being both relieved and depressed.

He was glad to have made the acquaintance of the notorious and much-feared weaver; and he had a happy feeling that the meeting with this man would not be without importance in his future work in the parish. But he was ashamed that he had not had the courage to talk openly to this man. What reason had he to suspect him? Certainly report did not speak to his credit — but then, in this instance, report only meant Provst Tönnesen, who could scarcely be called impartial on this subject. But what right had he to assume a hidden design behind his frankness?

He mentally recalled the whole conversation. But as, by so doing, he was again reminded by the weaver's strange words of his mother, his thoughts were all at once turned in another direction.

He had not often heard his mother mentioned since he had been grown up, and altogether he did not know much more about her than what he remembered to have seen himself. For several years he had felt that there was something in her early life which the family were anxious to hush up. What it was he had never been able to discover. After his mother's unhappy death — his young friends and companions had been afraid even of alluding to her in his presence; and he had had a natural shyness in speaking of her to strangers, especially as his father and his other relations always preserved absolute silence concerning everything connected with her. Only an aged aunt who lived in a convent had once, in a moment of excitement, said that he must never forget "how deeply his mother had offended the prejudices of her class." Now, the weaver's words and the pictures on the walls of the peasant's room pointed out distinctly what direction this "offence" had taken. The more he buried himself in recollections of her, and of her curious solitary life in his father's house, so much the more were the mists enveloping her image dispersed. He saw her before him with her hair dressed high, and the plain black gown which in his boyhood had always somewhat embarrassed him, because it so little resembled the dresses of the other ladies of their circle, who were also plainly a little oppressed by her presence. He remembered her private sitting-room, which was not in the least like the other rooms, and where she would often shut herself up for days without seeing anyone. Many a time as a child had he stood outside in the dusk, not knowing if he dared knock. When at last he summoned up courage to enter, he would see his mother crouching in one corner of the long horse-hair sofa, gazing fixedly before her as if she had not heard him. Only after he had stood by her side for some time and whispered "Mother," would she lay her hand on his head and silently stroke his hair; or she would take him on her knee and press him to her with passionate tenderness while she told him many tales of warriors and king's sons, who, under the banner of Christ, had gone forth into the world to fight for truth and the right — he also remembered that his brother and sister seldom visited their mother in her room, and generally fell asleep during her stories. They were younger, and amused themselves better in their father's handsome library with the picture books and the big globe. The servants also called them "the young lady and gentleman," while they nicknamed him "the mistress' boy." How often and how bitterly had he not felt, that since the day of his mother's death, he had become solitary and homeless in his father's house!

He wandered on the beach so long, buried in his thoughts, that he forgot both time and place. When at length he reached the Parsonage, he found to his dismay that the guests had already begun to arrive, and he had to hurry his dressing so as not to be too late.

When he entered the drawing-room a quarter of an hour later, he was received by a most ungracious look from the Provst, who, in evening dress and skull cap, was gesticulating in the middle of the room, in his animated conversation with a couple of other gentlemen, also in evening dress.

There were about a score of people assembled. The three landowners of the neighbourhood were there, the old schoolmaster Mortensen, Aggerbölle the veterinary surgeon, and Villing the store-keeper, and all their wives in silk dresses. In addition, there were six peasant farmers from Veilby, their wives, and Johanson, the young assistant teacher. There were none of the Skibberup people, and no representatives of the Veilby cottagers, because the last of the faithful among these had, to the Provst's great mortification, been drawn away to Hansen's Meeting House.

Two of the landowners were tall powerful men, as like each other as brothers, which they were not. The third was a little, peevish-looking fat man with a red patchy face and protruding eyes (like poached eggs swimming in fat). From his broad lower jaw, which stuck out from the upper part of his face like a trough, a grey beard  grew, covering an immense double chin which hung out over his neck like a paunch. He walked up and down with his hands behind him near the dining room door, grunting and looking impatiently at his watch every minute.

The six peasant women, all dressed alike in black stuff gowns and close-fitting caps embroidered with gold, sat silent in a row, along by the window, with their brown hands motionless on their laps, grasping folded pocket handkerchiefs. Their husbands, dressed in homespun, stood against the wall close to them, looking just as serious.

Jenson, the chairman of the parish council, with his purple turkey-like beak, was the only one quite at ease, and his voice rang out like that of a man accustomed to move in good society.

The ladies were seated in arm-chairs round the table in the middle of the room, their silk trains flowing over the carpeted floor. The tongues wagged merrily here, in that kind of conversation where no one knows either what they say themselves or what the others answer. The conversation was led by the wife of one of the landowners, a towering lady in green satin and white lace, who had just returned from a visit to Copenhagen, and was untiring in relating her experiences. The others eagerly echoed her praises of the extensions and improvements in the town. Only Mrs Mortensen, the portly wife of the schoolmaster, who had not been vouchsafed a visit to the capital for the last twenty years, sat pursing up her mouth in a contemptuous manner; and at last she protested loudly that she hated Copenhagen, and that for her part she would rather die than set her foot in it.

Her remarks called forth a perfect storm of opposition. They all turned towards her with "Dear Mrs Mortensen"; but she was not to be cowed, and repeated her words with conviction; and added that she certainly could not imagine how people could endure to live, even for a week, in such a babel and crowd.

In the meantime, the thin, shy, little Mrs Aggerbölle sat silently looking before her with an absent and worried expression, as if her thoughts were still with her home and children. She sat with her hands on her lap, looking ready to faint from fatigue and night watching. It looked as if she had carefully sought out a place behind Mrs Mortensen 's large person, so that the evening light should not fall too cruelly upon her prematurely aged features and faded silk gown — the old-fashioned cut of which, and the far too roomy bodice, bore sorrowful witness to bygone youthful charms. Now and then she glanced fearfully at her husband, who stood in a defiant attitude by the stove, as if disclaiming all knowledge of the smell of benzine which emanated from his shiny dress coat, and diffused itself all over that part of the room where he stood. He had only come home late in the afternoon from a peasant christening-feast in a neighbouring parish. Reminiscences of the night's carouse were plainly visible on the beardless parts of his face, in the shape of dark red patches, showing that the child had not been christened with water alone.

The young assistant teacher, Johansen, stood alone by the piano, with one leg lightly crossed over the other, the tips of the toes just touching the ground. He had a white glove on one hand, and a pocket handkerchief stuck in between his waistcoat and his vast shirt front.

Johansen, who had come to the parish about the same time as Emanuel, had quickly, in contrast to the other, become the lion of the neighbourhood. With his dark, somewhat theatrical hair, which, on grand occasions, was curled all over his head, his pale, fat, beardless face, his marvellously starched and frilled shirt, his stout legs and small feminine feet, he had fascinated all the young wives and girls at the winter festivities; his social talents had even procured admission for him to the country houses round about, and it was already considered not unlikely that one of the young ladies of the neighbourhood might one day bestow upon him something more than her admiration.

A moment after Emanuel's arrival the folding doors to the dining-room were thrown open. Miss Ragnhild came in and invited the company to sit down.

She was dressed in black silk, with yellow palm branches scattered over it, and a sort of lace overdress, which was transparent at the neck and below the elbows. Round her long, slender neck she wore a fine gold chain in four strands, gathered into an opal clasp. She had a large tortoise-shell comb in her dark auburn hair.

"Will the gentlemen please take ladies?" called out the Provst, himself offering his arm to the tall wife of the Squire.

A race took place among the elder gentlemen for Miss Ragnhild. Jensen, who was nearest to her, was the happy man, and he conducted her to the dining-room with uplifted nose.

Emanuel bowed to Mrs Aggerbölle, who remained behind when the other gentlemen had taken their ladies. The peasants took their own wives by the hand, and brought up the rear of the solemn procession in silence.

Chapter Ten

In the middle of the table, under a large hanging lamp, stood a tall epergne with flowers. There were tall, seven-branched candelabra at each end of the table. The napkins on each plate were in the shape of a bishop's mitre, under which a piece of bread was hidden. The table was spread with a collection of delicate viands. There was fish in different coloured jelly, birds stuffed with forcemeat, several kinds of salads in large blue glass bowls, lobsters and sardines in tins, besides a host of other things, all arranged with Miss Ragnhild's characteristic and refined taste.

Although the menu did not offer any surprises, as it was always much the same on these occasions, yet the festive appearance of the table and the unusual beauty of the china at once impressed the company favourably, and the meal began in solemn silence. The fat little landowner set to work immediately, with his elbows out, to ladle into his mouth voraciously, with knife and fork, whatever came near him.

Aggerbölle, on the other hand, struggled bravely against his evil tendencies. He sat for a long time with the same glass of claret before him, and never more than half-filled his plate, consequently he was able to glance at his wife with proud self-esteem, for he had solemnly promised her on the way to the Parsonage to behave with propriety and moderation.

At first the Provst was the only one, so to speak, who conversed; and altogether he shewed himself to be an equally amiable and entertaining host. He saw that the dishes were passed round, invited the gentlemen to fill their glasses, told little anecdotes, and, by the gallantry of his behaviour, disclosed the former "society" man, who was involuntarily stimulated and carried away by the sight of bright lights, flowers, and ladies in silk attire.

When the meal had proceeded for a quarter of an hour, he tapped his glass, and began an elaborate speech. Beginning with Solomon's proverb, he spoke in copious and polished terms of the strength felt in times of difficulty from knowing oneself to be surrounded by faithful friends. He expressed the hope that the circle he saw around him, all of the same party, "and also the peace of the congregation," might never be broken, and ended by heartily thanking the guests for the pleasure of their company.

Immediately afterwards, one of the tall, heavily built landowners rose, and expressed in fluent terms the thanks of the company to the Provst for his richly blessed activity in the parish. For a moment there was a danger of his touching upon some of the serious questions which the Provst had passed lightly over, by his throwing out a remark as to the "levelling tendencies of the age," against which the Provst was so powerful a bulwark. But sticking fast at this point, as if the flow of his words had come to an end, he concluded abruptly by proposing the health of the Provst and Miss Ragnhild.

After the company had again risen and touched glasses, the spirits rose considerably; and when at last the sweet course — a mighty plum-pudding — was put flaming upon the table, the satisfaction broke out into general mirth.

But now Aggerbölle's evil moment had arrived. Plum-pudding was one of his favourite dishes, and the decanters of heating wines also began to circulate. Then he was so unfortunate as to have a very bad example opposite to him, in the fat little Squire, who, during the whole meal, sat with the same peevish air, "gorging like a tapeworm" — as Aggerbölle later expressed himself — with all the daintiest dishes, so that he was actually forced to turn his eyes away, not to be led into temptation.

Now for the life of him he could no longer withstand. With a desperate and beseeching glance at his wife, he helped himself to a wedge of pudding, weighing at least a pound and a half, and directly after, tossed off two brimming glasses of sherry, as if at once to deafen himself to the voice of conscience.

Peals of laughter and loud conversation now resounded on all sides. Only the peasants remained silent. They sat all the time timidly trying the mysterious dishes, as if they were dead rats, and sipping the wine like medicine. One of them whispered to his neighbour, who was looking despondently at a piece of pudding which continued to blaze on his plate —

"If we on'y had one o' mother's dumplins now. These here made-up dishes can't be good for country folk's insides."

Emanuel was placed about half way down the long table. He had not talked much during the meal, and his companion, who was entirely taken up with keeping an eye on her husband, had not helped him much. He was disgusted by this empty and artificial entertainment.

The conversation with the weaver still rang in his ears, and through the haze of the lights, and the steam in the room, he still saw the sunny peasant's room with its simple air of comfort and sober Sunday festivity.

Miss Ragnhild, from the further end of the table, several times tried to attract his attention in order to drink a glass of wine with him. But he intentionally avoided her eye; because, of all the company present, she was the most displeasing to him. He considered that her dress was in questionable taste, nay, even shocking; and he noticed with shame how Johansen, who sat near her, absolutely devoured with his eyes her white neck and arms, which shone through the thin stuff, while he bent over her making pleasant remarks. Nor did she listen with indifference to this absurd caricature of a man about town. She lay back in her chair looking quite lively. The heat, the wine, and the sound of the many voices had brought a slight tinge of colour to her cheeks; and when she smiled, her eyes shone with excitement.

In his thoughts he compared her with the sober, healthy, rosy-cheeked peasant girl in whose company he had lately been, and who, in her simple dark red dress, seemed to him a hundred times prettier than any of these dressed up ladies in their flaunting dresses of silk and tulle. He glanced over the assembled company, from the Provst and the squires with their self-satisfied faces to the stolid row of peasants — and he thought how woefully he had been deceived. He — who at one time thought that he had fled from the abomination of culture for ever — now found that here he had only fallen into the arms of a ludicrous caricature of this same culture. Or was not this the same frivolity? The same arrogance? The same hypocrisy? They rose from table, and the company dispersed themselves in the various rooms. The ladies took possession of the drawing-room, while the gentlemen settled themselves in the study to smoke.

Miss Ragnhild met Emanuel at the dining-room door. "Velbekomme," she exclaimed merrily, giving him her hand. "All the same, I think you might have said, 'Tak for mad.' Or do you not consider my table worthy of praise? And why were you so wanting in gallantry as never even to look at me? I wanted to drink a glass of wine with you."

"Oh, I saw you very well. I thought Mr Johansen was very much taken up with you, and I could not find it in my heart to take you away from him."

"Poor Johansen," she laughed, "you are always down upon him. I admit he is very ludicrous, but, good heavens, he's a man after all, and he does not always talk about cattle and the price of corn. He is even a man of taste. I noticed to-day that he uses a scent which is not at all bad; and then he talked to me both about Wagner and Beethoven. What more can one want?"

"I daresay you are right, and in my opinion you and Mr Johansen suit each other admirably."

The tone of Emanuel's answer made the young lady draw herself up. She looked at him, and then said with displeasure —

"I think you forget yourself, Mr Hansted. It appears to me, altogether, that latterly you have begun in a deplorable degree to lose your former amiability."

"You are no doubt right on this point also, Miss Ragnhild. I feel myself, that I am out of place in this company, and I was just about to leave it when I met you. If your father asks for me, will you be so good as to make my excuses to him?"

He bowed stiffly and left the room. Miss Ragnhild remained on the threshold, thunderstruck, looking after him as he went.

·BOOK· ·THREE·

Book Three

Chapter One

One Sunday afternoon in May, the Meeting House in Skibberup was crammed with people, whose strained expectant faces plainly showed that something unusual was about to happen. It was indeed a remarkable day in the history of Skibberup. The speaker who was expected was no less a person than Provst Tönnesen's curate, Pastor Hansted.

Every seat in the long, dimly lighted room, (formerly a barn) was taken, and groups of men and lads hung round the windows blocking out what light there was. There was a lively buzz of gay and loud voices. It was plainly to be seen that it was no gathering of Veilby peasants; for though the distance between Veilby and Skibberup was not more than a couple of miles, the inhabitants of the twin villages were as different as if they did not belong to the same part of the country. This circumstance was not the result of chance, but was caused by the difference in position and conditions of life to which, in the course of time, the inhabitants had been subjected. While the peaceful inhabitants of Veilby had always busied themselves with ploughing and harvesting their wide acres since the time of Arild — Skibberup had been originally — and, to a certain extent, still remained — a fishing village, whose inhabitants chiefly maintained themselves by fishing. As lately as a couple of generations ago, the people of Skibberup looked upon the cultivation of the land as a minor affair to be left to the women, while the men paddled about in the fiords far and near, and made land journeys round the coast to dispose of their catches. Many tales were still told of the stirring adventures of the old Skibberup race both on land and at sea.

At one end of the room stood a simple reading desk, behind which the old brick wall of the barn was draped with a "Dannebrog" flag, which was so hung that the white cross on the red ground was upright.

The benches in front of the desk were almost entirely taken up by women, and the men ranged themselves at the back of the room and round the walls on both sides.

Else Anders Jörgen and her daughter Hansine were the objects of much attention among the company, as they took their seats on one of the middle benches. Else's plump face, with the light protruding eyes, her iron grey hair and large gold-embroidered cap, with broad red ribbons hanging down at one side, would have attracted attention in any assemblage; but the sensation which she made to-day was owing to the fact, known to all, that it was in her house, that the curate and the weaver had had the meetings in which the great event of to-day had originated. In a way it was considered that the happy ending of the affair was due to Else. She, not having been at home on the occasion of the first meeting between the curate and the weaver, and having heard on her return of its unfortunate issue, made up her mind on her own account to seek out Mr Hansted, for whom, in spite of all, she had preserved an unswerving affection since their first meeting by her daughter's sick bed. On the following Sunday, after the service, she went up to him outside the church, and asked him to renew his visit to her that same evening, "to meet a few good friends who very much wanted to talk to him." Mr Hansted accepted her invitation at once with alacrity, and as she had taken the precaution beforehand to ensure the presence of the weaver and a few other leading men of the village, a serious interchange of opinions at last took place between the curate and the congregation.

In consequence of these repeated visits to Anders Jörgen's house, and especially on account of the attention he had plainly shown Else and her daughter, in seeking them out after church every Sunday, and walking part of the way home with them, Hansine's friends had often teazed her about the curate, for whom, according to them, she had long cherished a secret affection. She certainly protested against the charge with great vehemence, and to-day, as if to prove her innocence of it, she was dressed, in contrast to all the other girls, in a plain dark green linsey dress without a bit of trimming or finery of any kind.

She looked well all the same — it was not for nothing that she was reckoned among the prettiest girls in the village; although the lower part of the face was childishly unformed, and a little out of proportion to the upper part, with the closely growing, dark eyebrows, and deep-set, earnest eyes. She sat with her usual almost unnaturally erect bearing, which gave to her trim little figure an air of self-confidence and power; and she neither took part in, nor listened to the gay chatter going on among the women round her. This want of sympathy with her surroundings was such an old story with her, that it no longer caused astonishment to any one. Even as a child, people had been amused by the comical "stand-off" air with which she met all advances of strangers, friendly or unfriendly. Her reserve had become more pronounced after she had been at a High School a few years ago; and while there, she had taken part in a "Friendly Meeting" in Copenhagen, where, among others, old Bishop Grundtvig spoke for the last time. Since then she had not been seen much outside her father's house and fields, more especially keeping away from the somewhat free and easy pleasures, in which the youth of the village indulged on Sundays and fine summer evenings. On the other hand, she was always to be heard singing at her work, in cow-byre and kitchen, or when walking over the fields with her milk pails.

The villagers sometimes laughed at her, but on the whole they did not pay much attention to these peculiarities. After all, she was little more than a child, only nineteen, and other girls in the neighbourhood who had been to High Schools were also observed to have peculiar ways. Besides, it was well known that it always took some time before the young people found their level again, and settled down to the simple every-day peasant life.

In the meantime, it was five o'clock, and the curate had not arrived. Some anxiety was apparent among a group of men, who had assembled at the door, with the weaver at their head, to receive him. They knew that latterly there had been strained relations between the Provst and his curate, since the former had become aware of the intercourse with the weaver and other prominent men of Skibberup. And now they feared that, notwithstanding all their precautions, Tönnesen should have heard of the meeting, and at the last moment prohibited Pastor Hansted from being present.

The weaver's pale face especially betrayed great uneasiness. He knew what was in store for him if the curate failed him to-day; but he also knew what enthusiasm would be aroused next day, when it became known that the Provst's colleague had been the speaker in his Meeting House.

Chapter Two

At last a solitary figure appeared on the sandbanks. It was Emanuel. He carried a light overcoat, and walked down to the village with hasty steps.

When he caught sight of the expectant group outside the Meeting House, he hurried forward and reached the door in a few minutes. His face, in spite of the heat and his hurried walk, was unusually pale, and betrayed a high state of nervous excitement, which gave him an utterly strange expression. He greeted the weaver and a few of the other bystanders absently, with a silent shake of the hand, and then immediately entered the hall.

Here the conversation was abruptly brought to a close, and all necks were craned to see him The weaver forced a way through the crowds with his long, baboon-like arms, and led him to the upper end of the room, where he offered him the place of honour, a basket chair with a broken seat.

After a few words had been exchanged between them, the weaver mounted the reading-desk and took a hymn-book from his coat-tail pocket. He remained standing a moment silent, with the book in his hands, while he closed one eye and glanced round the room with the other, a sly triumphant smile, dedicated to thoughts of the Provst, stealing over his face, which was answered gleefully by the men at the back of the room. At last he said in his guileless voice —

"Now, friends all, I suppose we must have a song to open with! Pastor Hansted has no partikler choice, so we can e'en please ourselves. What will ye have?"

Different songs were called for from the assemblage. At last they agreed on "Forward, peasants forward."

"Yes, let's sing that," said the weaver, with a meaning smile, "that'll just suit us."

He gave the note himself in a stentorian voice, and the other voices broke out deafeningly on all sides. It was not song. It was a wild enthusiastic shout, a delight in their own lung power, which threatened to blow the roof off.

Emanuel took his place on the basket chair, where he sat leaning forward with his legs crossed, running his hands uneasily through his hair from time to time. He did not join in the singing, and was not at all at his ease. The dark, gloomy room, the many free glances, and this noisy discordant singing, had for the moment put him out of spirits.

Besides which, he was a prey to conscientious scruples, because, on account of unavoidable circumstances, he had not had an opportunity of telling the Provst that he proposed to speak here to-day. He had intentionally put off till the last moment saying anything about it, just as he had asked the weaver not to announce the meeting publicly, so that the Provst might not have time to prohibit him from taking part in it. But when, shortly before leaving the Parsonage, he sought the Provst, he found that he had left the house half an hour earlier to pay a visit.

Under these circumstances he thought it proper to lay his plans before Miss Ragnhild, with whom he had made friends again since the collision on the night of the party; though the old familiar terms were by no means re-established. Miss Ragnhild was not nearly so surprised as Emanuel had expected. She had heard one thing and another about the curate's doings from the old servant; besides, she had guessed something of what was impending from various utterances of his own.

If Miss Ragnhild was not astonished, Emanuel — to make up — was very much so, at the unusual severity with which the young lady spoke home truths to him, and advised him strongly against taking his proposed step.

"With all your faint-heartedness you are a curiously fickle person," she said. "Here you plunge blindly into something you know nothing about — merely because you are not satisfied with the position in which you find yourself for the moment. I have no doubt it is ridiculous on my part to try to bring you to reason. I know what you are when you have got a thing into your head. But all the same, I will ask you seriously to consider, what may be the consequences of such a step, both to you and to us, Mr Hansted. When you know — and you do know — how this weaver and his imitators have behaved to my father, one would have thought it would be superfluous to point out to you how peculiar — to put it mildly, and not to say downright improper — any approach to these people must appear, and in fact is."

Without giving him time to answer, she turned and left the room.

These words, and the tone in which they were spoken, caused the last scales to fall from Emanuel's eyes. He had by no means been blind to what the consequences might be in the Parsonage, and he was quite prepared for his days there as the Provst's curate, being numbered. But he had thought that people would at any rate respect his serious convictions — nay, he had even entertained a faint hope that the storm might end in mutual reconciliation. He now saw that every attempt to come to an understanding would be fruitless; that hereafter, not only at the Parsonage, but among all "right thinking" people, both here and everywhere else, he would be looked upon as a traitor, to whom no mercy would be shewn.

It was therefore doubly painful to him, to have appeared to keep silence towards the Provst, in a way which might be considered cowardly.

Besides making him clearer sighted, this new collision with Miss Ragnhild had roused in him the self-confidence and readiness for battle which hitherto he had lacked. Now he only felt eager to break with his past once and for all. Even at this moment, when he was depressed by the discomfort of the gloomy room and the lack of solemnity among the assemblage, he was burning with impatience to arrive at a settlement, to leave the bridge behind him, and to take the step which would put his position beyond all ambiguity.

As soon as the song came to an end he rose and mounted the reading-desk.

Chapter Three

He had purposely not prepared his address beforehand. He wanted to try for once to depend upon the inspiration of the moment, and use the words dictated by his heart — so as to avoid the stiff, artificial methods

70

which, according to old models, he had accustomed himself to use in his carefully written sermons.

All the same he did not come unprepared. The subject on which he had chosen to speak, had, on the contrary, for some time occupied his mind to an extraordinary extent. He had made up his mind to follow the advice the weaver gave him at their first interview, and talk to them about himself. He would try to draw a rough sketch for them of the life of a town-bred child during its growth, and give an account of the impressions to which such a child was subjected, so as to show them the conditions of life and the influences which had operated on his own development, and which had at last brought him to the parting of the ways where he now stood.

He began by telling them a little story. It was the story of a young princess who was one day presented with a lovely flower by a lover. She was at first delighted with it, and was about to fasten it in her bosom. But when she discovered that the flower was no artificial imitation of nature, made of silk or painted feathers, but a real, living rose, she threw it aside angrily, and told her maid to sweep the ugly peasant's flower away at once.

This story, he said, seemed to him, applied to our times, to contain a deep and sad truth. In our time it was not alone the young, spoiled princess who thus scornfully rejected the flowers of life — no, the whole so-called modern culture, in its progress in the large towns, was an acknowledged struggle to corrupt God's earthly gifts, an arrogant attempt to change — or, as it was called — "to develope and improve" God's works on earth, and to create a universe according to the poor capacity of mankind. One had only to look at any of the large towns, or to think how people in the chief cities of the world herded together in hundreds of thousands like a new Tower of Babel, and did their best with coal dust, high houses, and tall chimneys to shut out God's sun and the fresh air — and one could not fail to see how the whole of this Society was built up in antagonism to Nature.

Or if one looked at persons — at these dressed up ladies who, by means of all kinds of machines — "crinolines, corsets," or whatever the things were called — "improved" their appearance; if one looked at men, old and young, who got themselves up according to the latest Paris fashions, and by the help of pomades, wax, and hot irons robbed their hair and beards of every natural line. In fact, in great as in small things, one could not but notice this triumphant rebellion against the laws of nature.

Or if one went from the streets into the houses, and sought these people in their 'occupations, their recreations, their joys and their sorrows — everywhere one saw how modern civilization, in tearing mankind away from the ever-youthful mother, Nature, had doomed them to a world of show and an existence of shams, which in the end they fancied to be the only true and real one. The tired workmen who in the evening sought the beer shop to procure a moment's artificial pleasure by means of the glass; the young ladies who at dusk seated themselves at the piano to conjure up the spirit of moonlight, the roaring of waves, or the song of the lark within four walls; all those who, in

71

the stifling heat and pestilent air of the theatre, shed tears over paid buffoons parodying human joys and sorrows among painted scenes; the "lover of Art," who best enjoyed the sight of a raging sea or a flowery meadow framed and glazed on his wall — were not all these like the princess who preferred the painted feather to the living, scented rose?

"And yet" — he continued — "this is only the least important outer side of the case. If we look deeper into modern life, if we look for the inner life behind this ugly mask — what do we see? We see humanity divided by a great gulf, which separates — not the good from the bad, not the honest from the dishonest, the children of God from the slaves of sin, — no, but the rich from the poor, the classes who live only for pleasure, from the needy and the suffering. On one side we have the masses toiling in poverty, on the other we have a chosen few living in idleness and profusion. Here — cold, darkness and ignorance reign; there — light, splendour and satiety. In this way the culture of to-day carries out Christ's law of brotherhood among men! Thus has it fulfilled the law, Love your neighbour! And the higher the state of culture in a community so much the wider the gulf; the louder the wails here, the bolder the licence there — until we, in the capitals, the so-called centres of culture, see the whole community in a wild state of moral dissolution, and hear voices from both sides melting into one vast uniform cry: the cry of the dying for air!"

He felt the need of making his point of view clear to his hearers at once; and a craving to confess openly the view of life which the solitude and self-absorption of the last few months had rooted in him. When he had once touched on his old subject of contention, he was urged on as if by a storm; the words surged to his lips with a fluency and ardour which surprised himself.

He felt perfectly well that it was the sting in Miss Ragnhild's words which cut him to the heart and inspired his passion, — and that it was her public challenge which called forth this veiled answer. To this was added the solemn silence around him, the long rows of strained listening faces. He did not feel here — as he did in church — any cold abyss between himself and his hearers. For the first time he felt the intoxication, which lies in seeing the thoughts of hundreds, held by the power of his words, the eyes of hundreds hanging on his lips. Going on in a lighter vein, he touched upon the restlessness of town life in all its forms; giving among other things a sketch of the long dinners, with course after course, and an endless variety of wines.

Then he spoke of the style of conversation prevalent at these entertainments. He who had the power of handling every subject on heaven and earth in a light and joking manner was said to have conversational talent; and by this alone was a person's worth gauged in the social world. To speak seriously on serious subjects — to inquire into the ardent longings and the higher aspirations of men was considered unsuitable and pedantic. In like manner it was contrary to good form to speak of one's own purposes in life, our plans and hopes, though it was quite the thing to chatter glibly about the latest scandal, dress and theatres.

"In this fevered atmosphere, amid this devouring restlessness," he went on, "our young people grow up. Amid frivolity, arrogance, twaddle and hypocrisy they receive the first deep impressions which are of such enormous importance in their future life. There is so much to be pruned, bent, ground, and polished before a child from the Almighty's workshop can become a presentable member of Society. Look at our young men, the youths who are to be our leaders, teachers, and judges! Before they reach their twentieth year, most of them have given up every higher and nobler aspiration, and have thrown overboard all faith in the true and fruitful Powers of life. They have learnt that Society only requires from them an irreproachable exterior, correct behaviour, and a pleasant smile; that a well-starched shirt-front is the shield to make them invulnerable in the battle of life; and that well-dressed hair, good clothes, and a twirled moustache are the passports to a happy and brilliant future. 'A hopeful youth' is the one who most easily learns the hypocrisies of Society, while the 'Bete noire' of the family is he whose whole nature revolts against these dictates of Society, and who defends himself with hands and feet against the poison which both at home and at school is dropped into eyes and ears." He pulled himself up. He perceived that the bitter memories of his own home had got the mastery over him, and he required a moment's pause to recover himself. When he looked at his watch he discovered to his horror that the time had flown, he had spoken for an hour and a quarter. "We shall have to stop," he said with an apologetic smile; and although on all sides he was begged to continue, he decided to break off.

"No, I think it's best to stop now. In any case I could not finish to-day what I want to say to you. But if we can agree to meet here again on another Sunday, I will continue then."

"Yes, yes," was shouted from all sides.

"Very well, send a message to me, and I shall be at your service. I will only add now that whatever my position in the parish in future may be — and possibly a change will take place from to-day — I feel sure that when once we have learnt to know and understand one another, that our common life will be happy and blessed. If these hours can contribute to that end, my aims will be accomplished."

Bowing slightly, he left the rostrum.

Chapter Four

A RUSTLE of clothes and a hum of voices went through the room as he finished. They were quite overcome with pleasure and surprise. The most sanguine of them had never in their wildest dreams hoped for such freedom of speech. But the hints in the curate's last words threw a vague gloom over their spirits. It had not occurred to them before that this meeting might have far-reaching consequences. They all looked towards the weaver, who at last pulled up his long limp figure from the end of a bench in the front row, and slowly entered the rostrum. He expressed the thanks of the meeting for the "stimulating" address in a remarkably few and dry words, and then proceeded — according to the usage of meetings — to ask the audience if any one wished to make any remarks on the discourse, "that is to say, if Mr Hansted has no objection," he added, turning with a smile to Emanuel, who silently shook his head.

"Well, then, anybody can address the meeting," he said, waving his hand towards the audience.

Immediately a figure on one of the middle benches started up, a little, ugly, poorly dressed woman, whose appearance roused a general commotion. Some even began to hiss, and shout "sit down." But she was evidently used both to appearing in public and to meeting opposition. Without paying the slightest attention to the disturbance, in an almost inaudible voice, like the mewing of a cat in a bag, and shewing absolutely toothless gums, she began, aided by mechanical gestures with her claw-like hand, to put a string of questions to the curate, whom she persisted in calling "the last honourable speaker." All that the curate had said was maybe very right and fine, she began. But what she wanted to know was, what he thought of the laws on taxation, and the new school orders. And she wished to know how the honourable speaker was disposed to the introduction of the new appendix to the hymn-book, and whether he thought it right that a man with fourteen cows should not let his labourers have a bit of grazing in the ditches. And she also wanted to know what he thought of the doctrine of Damnation, the Peace question, and old age annuities.

The disturbance among the people rose higher, and all eyes were again turned to the weaver, who appeared to be closely contemplating the sole of his boot.

When the hisses became universal, and completely drowned the speaker, he looked up with a broad smile, and rose.

"Come, come, now, Maren Smeds, hadn't we better keep all this here for another time. Seems like we shouldn't spoil the good impression of Mr Hansted's speech with too much jaw after it.

"Hear, hear," was heard on all sides.

The weaver, who seemed as if he would have added something more, stopped suddenly and sat down. At the same time, a dozen hands pulled Maren by the skirts down on to the seat with a bump like a wooden doll.

Emanuel, who had risen, looked with uncomprehending glances both at the speaker and at the hissers, when a bystander whispered a few words to him, and he sat down again.

Now a movement arose in the background. A man jumped on to the last bench, and in a loud voice asked leave to speak. It was the big, black bearded "Viking" figure, whom Emanuel had occasionally met before, first, as the speaker among the snow-clearers on that winter evening's sledge ride to Skibberup.

With a voice which rang through the room like a horn, he said:

"I'd like to thank the Pastor for what he's said to-day, too — but most of all for his presence. I think we can all say that we've found the man we wanted, and we weren't far wrong when we were pleased at hearing who was to be our curate. May be we haven't all been sure about it before, — I'll only say the curate must excuse it — but we've got our eyes open now as to what he really is, so I thank him heartily."

"Hear, hear," came from all the young men in the tightly packed windows and round the walls, while the women nodded approvingly.

"I'd just like to say, too, if, on account of this day, any troubles or unpleasantness come to the curate up there — I've said enough — there's room for a parson down here among us! If Mr Hansted gets into difficulties up there — isn't it so, friends? — we're quite ready to receive him with open arms and a big hurrah! Shall we pledge our words on it, eh?"

Thundering cheers from the windows and walls, nay, even from the women, followed these words.

Emanuel rose, his expression shewed that the "Viking's" clarion had roused him too. He stood by the rostrum, and immediately all was hushed. He stood for a moment, as if fighting out something with himself. Then he said in a firm but low voice:

"I thank you for your sympathy, my friends. It makes me happy and contented. Nobody knows what the future will bring, but I no longer have any fear." Raising his voice, he added, the colour mounting to his cheek, "I know my vocation, and neither opposition nor battle — nothing shall hinder me from following it. Be sure of that! In thanking you all for your goodwill, I will ask you to join me in singing the beautiful old hymn, 'All lies in God our Father's hand!'"

The song was sung, and then another, and several people called for one more, but then the weaver rose and abruptly declared the meeting closed.

It was long past seven. The room was almost dark, and the atmosphere stifling. It became a little lighter when the men sprang down from the windows — some outwards, others in. The meeting broke up in a red glow from the setting sun, and the people pressed towards the door with a deafening noise.

Emanuel was surrounded on his way out by people who wanted to shake hands and to thank him. The devotion of the people overwhelmed him with thankfulness. There was a perfect hum of delight and admiration around him. "What a handsome young man!" "Yes, he's a child of grace!" "So pious and good!" "They say he's so like his poor mother, too!"

At the entrance he was met by Else, who came up to him, and pressed his hand with much emotion, while child-like tears of joy stood in her clear eyes. He smiled and said, "Thank you, Else!" and looked round for Hansine. But she was not there. It was a little disappointment to him in the midst of his pleasure. Although he had not seen her, he felt sure she must have been there.

Chapter Five

At this moment the "Viking" came up to him, and introduced himself as Nielsen, the carpenter. With a complacent, but bright and pleasant smile, which showed his white teeth, he said, after Emanuel had thanked him for his remarks:

"Perhaps it would amuse Mr Hansted to go to the shore with us? We generally go there after the meetings, and sing songs and talk to each other, when it's fine enough. To-night it's real summer weather, as we say, so we'd be glad if you'd honour us with your company, sir."

Emanuel accepted the invitation with pleasure. He had no desire to leave his new friends and return to the parsonage. "That will be delightful! What a lot of people there are here to-day," said he, letting his eyes rove over the tightly packed groups. Again he looked about for Hansine. He could not believe that she was not there.

It was soon whispered from group to group that the curate was going with them.

The announcement hastened the movements of those who had children to attend to, or cattle to fodder at home, before they could go. Even "old Erik" might be seen hobbling away with his Sunday crutch, to look after his cat at the other side of the village pond in which a flaming sunset sky was reflected.

A crowd of young people, girls and youths, had already started for the rendezvous on the north shore; the girls first, arm in arm, singing, and the youths behind in twos and threes, with lighted pipes and cigars. The elders soon followed, mostly in pairs, labouring up the steep path which led over the sandhills.

A couple of elderly men had joined Emanuel — two brisk little figures of the usual Skibberup type, with long arms and short legs. They were both leading persons, and tried their best to get Emanuel to say what he thought the Provst would say to "this here business," and how he thought he would get on in the future.

But Emanuel constantly turned aside from the subject. He felt the need of rest for his spirit and his thoughts for this evening, and of enjoying these few short hours of happiness, and freedom unalloyed. Besides, he thought the evening far too fine for laying plans of war. It was as if nature herself urged an hour's peace and reconciliation. So he often stopped, and compelled the men to silence by looking around him, with outbursts of delight. The pure harmonious colouring of the sky was reflected in the glowing earth! Not a breath of air, not a sound. Yes! high, high up, under the flaming sky, a little lark, invisible, warbled to the setting sun — one sound in the infinite silence, a single quivering note, distant, and yet, at the same time, curiously near — like the twinkling of a solitary star.

When they reached the top of the hill, they saw the young people a couple of hundred paces ahead; they had seated themselves on a flowery strip of meadow by the wayside, but now they started on again singing. Suddenly a little shiver ran through Emanuel. In the rear of the party he caught sight of her for whom he had been looking all the time — Hansine. She was walking arm in arm with a tall, strong, redhaired girl, in whom he recognised the gamekeeper's adopted daughter, Ane, Hansine's dearest friend, whom he had always seen with her in church. A little, thirr, shabby figure hung on her other arm, whose black dress, all too long, and boyish stride, plainly marked the newly confirmed. [1] Ane's brick-red hair was covered with a little straw hat trimmed with tartan ribbon, which looked as if it was meant for a child. Her dark green linsey dress was the same as Hansine's, and she had a bright yellow handkerchief round her neck, hanging in a three corner down her back. Hansine had a low, broad-brimmed, brown straw hat, but no handkerchief down her back; her black hat-ribbons reached her waist, which was encircled by the bright leather belt, the distinctive mark of every High School girl.

It looked as if the gamekeeper's daughter had kept the other two back to impart some important piece of news to them.

The little girl in black was bending forward, almost doubled up, to look her friend in the face, as if by so doing she could draw out the words with her eyes. Hansine, on the other hand, appeared only to hear with one ear. She was looking down, or to one side, as if wishing to hide her inattention. When they passed a flower by the wayside, which she could reach without letting go her friend's arm, she stooped and picked it.

Emanuel observed these trifles while absently answering the questions of the two peasants concerning the Provst and the future.

His eyes hardly left Hansine. He could not explain to himself what it was that interested him so strongly in this young girl, whom, in a way, he hardly knew at all. An impenetrable taciturnity always came over her in his presence, and altogether he had only spoken two or three times to her, and then merely on indifferent subjects. On his visits to her home she had always sat silent, half turned away, on the end of the bench under the window, without ever looking up from her work; but there was something in her curiously introspective character — in her glance, shy and defiant at the same time — yes, even in the reserve with which she armed herself in his presence, which impressed him with an almost awe-inspiring sense of her purity of soul, depth of feeling and uprightness.

As soon as he saw her he tried to hurry on his companions. He longed to speak to her, and, if possible, to discover by her face what impression his speech had made upon her. But it was difficult to get the two peasants out of their very leisurely walk, and before they reached the young girls, they had started running down the last steep slope to the shore.

A few minutes later, Emanuel and his companions also reached the meeting-place. This was a sandy spot close to the water, a semi-circular widening of the otherwise narrow shore which ran up between two steep cliffs. It was called "the church" by the country people, because they maintained that it was like an apse. An old tarred boat was hauled up on the beach, and the girls had already taken their places in closely packed rows on the thwarts and gunnel; while the youths were encamped on the sands. Hansine and her friends had got seats on the further end of the boat's prow towards the water, which was still rather rough after the wild weather of the previous day. The collection of different-coloured

dresses and bright summer hats, looked quite picturesque against the white sand and the deep blue waters touched with sunset tints.

By degrees all the rest of the company arrived and took their places on the slopes. Last of all — and greeted with acclamations — came old Erik hobbling down the steep path with his crutch, his bad foot in all its wrappings, looking like a baby in swaddling clothes.

Emanuel left his companions and seated himself higher up the slopes, feeling the need of a moment's quiet.

As he sat there, and saw couple after couple slowly wandering down towards the shore — always woman with woman, and man with man, and saw how they all stopped at the foot of the path to look for seats, as if dazzled by the light from sky and sea — he was reminded of the name of "Church," which the people had given to this spot. He had a feeling himself, at this moment, of having been witness to a church-going more solemn than any he had ever before taken part in. At last the whole congregation sat in long rows around him on the terraced slopes — the women lowest down with their skirts gathered round them, and pocket-handkerchiefs in their hands; some wore large black "church hoods," others their gorgeous gold-embroidered caps, which shone round their heads like halos in the fading light. The men sat in rows above them resting their elbows on their knees. Quite at the top, a

78

group of children lay with their hands under their cheeks, peeping down —
like the angels' heads in old altar pieces.

The church-like impression was strengthened when a hush came over the
people. The girls in the boat began to sing. With their arms round each other's waists, and faces turned to the sea, they sang a pious old evening hymn.

> The horse is stalled upon the close of day,
>   At eve each creature seeks its own retreat,
> The birds sit hushed upon the leafy spray,
>   And Reynard steals away with noiseless feet.
>
> Athwart the golden cloudbanks in the West,
>   God's portal stands by glowing sunbeams riven,
> And thither toil-worn spirits seek their rest
>   Within the all-embracing lap of Heaven.
>
> Oh, timorous soul, that by some hidden road
>   Seekest to rest thee till the break of light,
> Why dost forbear to enter God's abode,
>   And there disarm the terrors of the night?
>
> That gracious God, who, with his fostering care,
>   For every little bird hath made a nest
> And warmly lined it, shall He not prepare
>   A home, where homeless souls may safely rest.
>
> Knock! and the angel host shall let thee in,
>   Though full of fears, though sinful, though alone,
> And they will ease the burden of thy sin,
>   And lead thee to the Heavenly Father's Throne."

[1] Confirmation marks the line between childhood & womanhood very sharply.

Chapter Six

The singing sounded well in the clear, quiet spring evening. In the
open air, the voices lost the harsh tone they had under the low roof of the
Meeting House. It was as if the wide space gave them depth; as if heaven and
earth lent them their colours. Then they sang various national airs, in which
the others gradually joined. Then a powerful man's voice called for "The
death of young Buré."

"The death of young Buré! ...The death of young Buré!" was eagerly repeated on all sides, while the young men raised themselves to sitting pos-
tures.

Ane — Hansine's red-haired friend — was chosen to lead. She sat out at the very end of the boat like a figure head, and began to sing in a high powerful voice, which reminded one of the bright tints of her hair. The whole party sang the chorus, in which the girls came in as seconds. Nielsen the carpenter stood in the middle of the sandy place with legs astride, beating time with his arms, while he led the chorus in smiling enthusiasm, his teeth gleaming through his dark Viking beard.

"'Twas long ere the sun was yet in the south,
    In the early dawn,
That Sir Buré kissed Dame Inger's mouth.
    Heigh ho! but the morn is gay!

Sir Buré he saddled his ganger gray,
    All dapple-gray;
Dame Inger gazed down from her window all day.
    Heigh ho! but the Woods are green!

Then he hoisted his sail to the top of the mast,
    His silken sail,
And Sir Buré was borne on the blue waves so fast.
    Heigh ho! but 'tis heavy to part."

There were twenty odd verses in all; when the last was sung, the girls jumped off the boat and all the men clapped their hands.

"Perhaps you don't know that song, sir," said a young man with a fair beard and smiling face, who, together with a few other young men, sauntered up to Emanuel to open a conversation with him. "It's a sort of favourite with the young folks here, because it was written by our own High School director over in Sandinge. You may have heard tell of him. I daresay he's known all over the country."

Emanuel remembered very well having heard Sandinge High School spoken of as the place which the youth of the neighbourhood frequented, under the weaver's direction, when they wished to reach a higher intellectual development than the village school afforded; so he moved nearer to the three peasants, to hear something more about these peculiar teaching institutions which had gained so much ground in the country in the last few years, and which he had often wished to know better.

He then heard to his great astonishment that Sandinge was barely six miles off, a short distance from the opposite shore. They could plainly see the heath-clad hills, behind which the town was hidden, from the place where they sat. The man with the fair beard was himself a former pupil, and gave such a glowing account of the life and teaching at the school, that Emanuel was quite anxious to make the acquaintance of this man, and made up his mind to visit him at no distant date.

In the meantime, baskets of provisions were brought out by the married women, some of the girls handed sandwiches on the lids of baskets or dock leaves, while others went about with bottles of milk. The carpenter took charge of a jar of small beer, and altogether acted as master of the ceremonies, while the weaver, on the other hand, sat in elevated retirement on a tuft of grass, talking to a couple of old women.

After supper the girls and the young men took to playing games and dancing to their own singing.

Emanuel, who had again remained alone, sat with his cheek resting on his hand, looking down on this scene with a half absent smile. The merry voices of the young people carried his thoughts over the water — and further away.

He thought of the home of his childhood, and his own joyless youth, and of all his dreams. He felt now — that he was in the midst of the realization of those dreams. This was the joyous mirth of childhood at which he had dimly guessed. Here was the Promised Land, for whose milk and honey he had yearned.

His eye sought Hansine. He only found her after considerable search among a little group of older girls, who were not taking part in the dancing, but stood by the boat looking on. She was sitting behind the others on the gunnel, with her head half turned away, gazing fixedly at a distant point of the water, as if the notes of the singing had led her thoughts, too, on distant travels. The twilight was considerably advanced, and her features were not plainly visible at the distance where Emanuel was. But the outline of her figure was all the more plainly marked against the purple water. His eye followed the lines of her profile, and the powerful curves of the upper part of her figure — and a fear arose in him — a fear that, from one cause or another, she might have something against him. Otherwise he could not understand why she had so carefully avoided him all day, to the extent of not even coming near him. Had she, perhaps, been disappointed in his discourse? He had really spoken several times, with her alone in his mind, and his wish had all along been that she, above all others, should understand him. Was it possible that she was the only one not to be touched by his words?

His disturbed expression was noticed by some of the old people, who at once remarked upon it to some of the others. As they thought he might disapprove of the dancing, they passed the word to stop it. Besides, the evening

81

was so far advanced that it was time to break up. A cold mist was rising from the ground and the stars were out.

A few old people rose and began to take leave, then others followed their example. They were on the whole a little disappointed that Emanuel had not spoken, or told a story or suchlike. Old Erik, who had sat at his feet — like a true disciple — had looked up, every time there was a moment's silence, into Emanuel's face, with a happy expectant expression, like a child who hopes to have the whole world of elves and fairies unfolded to him. But all the same they went and shook hands with him, and thanked him heartily for his company.

Only Hansine took her red-haired friend by the arm as soon as the company broke up, and disappeared with her along the shore, to walk part of the way home with her to the "Gamekeeper's Lodge," as the country people complacently called the humble cottage provided for the overseers, in a little wood, in the southern corner of the parish.

Chapter Seven

A FEW minutes later Emanuel stood on the top of a hill over which a path ran northwards to Veilby. He took off his broad-brimmed hat and covered his eyes with his hand, while he listened to the distant voices of the people who were singing as they wandered homewards.

The last notes died away. He was alone. Round about him lay the earth steeped in the silence of the desert. Over his head was the mighty dome of heaven with the pale light of the shimmering stars. Inexorable silence reigned, as if all nature were turned to stone.

He felt as if he had all at once been shut out of a shining Paradise...He turned his unwilling eyes towards Veilby, where in the distance he saw the high-lying Parsonage garden looming like a dark, threatening bank of clouds against the last faint streaks of light. There, reckoning, strife, and excommunication awaited him!

He walked on a few steps, but felt so tired and worn out that he was obliged to sit down on a stone by the wayside. The oppression which he had kept under by force all the evening, now, in this solitude, got complete mastery over him, crushing him like a wild beast let loose. It was not that he repented what he had done. He only felt so bitterly alone, so homeless, so forsaken! There was no longer a single place in the world that he could call his own, — not one creature to give him comfort or support. If he even had a home, where he could find rest and peace after the struggle; had he but a good and faithful wife, who would share his victory and his defeat — it would then have been the joy of his life to fight for freedom and happiness. But this was struggling on a bare heath with empty hands. No comfort, never a refuge!

He sat for a time gazing into space, with one name ever on his lips...Hansine! Then he tore himself away from the thought. Dreams! he whispered, and rose. He stood for a moment looking down at the Fiord, which was now wrapped in light, grey mists. Then he slowly continued his walk.

But he could not banish the thought of Hansine. It was as if all his restlessness, depression, and fears at last resolved themselves into this one question: Why does she shun me? What is there in me to repulse her? ... It seemed to him, more and more, that the answer to this contained an omen for his whole future; in this state of uncertainty he was in no condition to open battle. He stopped.

He must have certainty this very night. He remembered having seen Hansine go along the shore with her friend. She must therefore come back. She would hardly take the short cut to the village, across the bogs and the water courses. She would consequently come back to the meeting place. He would still be able to meet her there, and talk to her without being disturbed; make her tell him what she had against him, why she avoided him, what he had done to her...

He turned and retraced his steps. Fearful of being too late, he hurried on stumbling over every stone in the dim light, and in a few minutes found himself in the "church" again.

All at once he stopped and his heart ceased to beat — there she was, coming towards him, not a hundred paces off, curiously big in the dusk, melting away like a shadow into the misty Fiord. She was walking close to the water, quite slowly — like one who had longed for solitude — singing softly and gazing out over the Fiord.

Suddenly she stopped and pressed her hands to her heart — she had seen him.

He approached quite slowly, so as to give her time to recognise him; and when he reached her, he raised his hat.

"Don't be afraid, Hansine, ...you see it is only me. I hope I do not disturb you. I shan't do you any harm, you may be sure."

These last words slipped out involuntarily on seeing her alarm. She stood as if turned to stone. Her face was ashy pale, her eyes, under their dark eyebrows, fixed on him with a curious startled gaze.

In his helplessness he gave an elaborate explanation of his presence. He said that he had seen her go with her friend; and as he had not been able to speak to her all day, he had decided to go and meet her and have a little talk with her.

She remained standing like a dumb creature, and did not stir from the spot. Her face was as immoveable as a mask, and she stared at him with her half shy, half threatening glance, like a wounded doe.

"My dear Hansine!" he exclaimed. "You can never be angry with me for stopping you. I can assure you, you need not have the least fear of me. I only wanted to say "How-d'yedo" to you, and anybody might listen to what I have to say, for that matter. I suppose you don't doubt that?"

Still she did not speak.

The blood rushed to Emanuel's cheeks. Was it possible that she really distrusted him? The thought seemed too ridiculous, but he saw that he had acted somewhat thoughtlessly in seeking her at this hour, and in such a solitary spot. So he tried to make a joke of it.

All the same there was a touch of bitterness in his voice as he said:

"Well, I really think that I am in your way. You must excuse me, ...that was far from my intention. To tell the truth, it did not occur to me that time and place were not well chosen. But, good heavens! am I not your priest...I had hoped that we were too good friends to misunderstand each other! Well — good-night then! I suppose you are not afraid to shake hands with me?"

She slowly gave him her hand, but drew it quickly back again, and with a short "goodnight," turned away and went back the way she came.

Emanuel remained standing, dumb with astonishment. He had felt how cold her hand was, and how it shook. What in the world was the matter with her?

"Hansine!" he called.

She appeared not to hear him, and hurried on.

"Hansine!" he called, this time with the full power of his voice, and then she stopped as if bereft of power.

He went along to her, and although her back was to him, he saw at once that she was struggling to keep herself from crying.

"But what has happened?" he exclaimed in alarm.

The sound of his voice roused her, and she tried to fly. But he took hold of her arm and held her back.

"No, no, you mustn't go away like this. Whatever is the matter, Hansine? Has any one done you any harm? Won't you confide in me? I assure you I am your friend."

She tried to wrench herself away, but he put his arm round her shoulder and held her fast.

"I will not let you go in this state. You are not master of yourself. For heaven's sake, Hansine, what is it?"

He was at his wits' end. Was she ill? He did not hear any sound of crying, but he was sensible that the form he held was convulsed with emotion. What on earth should he do?

He had tears of sympathy in his eyes. He could not bear to see her suffer so. His own spirit was in such a turmoil that he could hardly command himself. Now for the first time he felt certain what his feelings were for this young girl. He knew it now — he loved her! For the first time in his life he felt love flame up in his heart and take possession of all his senses. He loved her!

84

He felt with all his soul that it was she of whom he had dreamt in his youth, whom he had yearned for all his life!

"Loose me! ...Let me go!" she cried hoarsely between her teeth.

But he held her fast. If it had cost him his life he could not have let her go.

"Hansine!" he said in a voice which was meant to be calm, but he strove in vain to conceal his own passionate emotion.

"Can I not comfort you in any way? Have you no confidence in me? — Are you angry with me? — You must tell me that, I have thought about nothing else all day, because you would not speak to me, ...and I have wanted so much to see you. Are you angry with me? If you would only answer that question, I would let you go. Do you hear, Hansine? you must not go before you have told me that. Are you angry with me?"

"No, let me go!"

But he did not loosen his hold. Something in her voice, and the wild beating of her heart, which he felt right up his arm, all at once enlightened him. Had he been blind? Was it possible that she, too — The thought surged through his brain like a raging wind, and he became quite dizzy. He forced himself to be calm for fear of frightening her. Trembling, he bent over her and said: "Hansine, you must answer one more question. You must not be angry ...but am I right in feeling that we have been brought together this evening by God Himself? You must not hide anything from me. Do you care for me? Tell me...Do you care for me ever so little?"

She put forth all her strength to try and get away, and uttered a muffled cry. But now both his arms were round her, and he drew her to him with ungovernable passion.

"Is it true? Hansine ...dear, dear Hansine, do you love me a little?

She no longer heard anything. She had sunk powerless in his arms, and her tears could no longer be restrained, she cried so violently that she was quite convulsed. She was paralysed with shame and despair. She seemed as if she would fall to the earth, and implore it to open and hide her.

"Then, then, do not cry any more, dearest one. It's all right now, isn't it? Come, we will go home together, and talk to your [1] parents...

Come."

These words roused her.

"You must not go with me," she said quickly, passing her hand over her tear-stained eyes.

"But why not? don't you want any one to see us until I have spoken to your parents? Well, perhaps you are right. Then we part here ... it has got late. Good-night, then, Hansine! But to-morrow I shall come to you; then we will have a good talk together."

She was turning to leave him, when, with a beseeching voice, he called her back.

"You won't leave me without saying 'goodbye,' will you?"

She turned round and gave him her hand mechanically. He took it in both his and pressed it tenderly to his lips. Then her tears and despair broke out afresh; she turned quickly and hurried away.

He stood a moment irresolute. Was he really to leave her like this.

He followed her.

"Hansine, ...had I not better go with you."

"No, no," she said passionately, and stamped her foot.

He did not understand her, but he followed no further.

"Well, then, I will come to-morrow," he called after her, "and then I shall see a smile on your face again, shall I not?"

She did not answer, he only heard her inconsolable sobs, while, almost running, she disappeared over the hills. When Emanuel turned back to the beach a few minutes later, he was disagreeably surprised to see a man in a light overcoat, standing a little way off leaning on a stick. He immediately recognised Johansen, and saw that, according to his usual custom, he had been wandering among the hills, on the look out for solitary girls.

He decided to appear as if he did not see him. But Johansen raised his hat, and shouted: "A lovely evening, Mr Hansted; it's perfect summer weather."

[1] He here passes from the formal "you" to the "thou" of engaged people.

Chapter Eight

The next morning a heavy thunder cloud rested over Veilby Parsonage. When Emanuel, somewhat later than usual, came down to breakfast, he found neither the Provst nor Miss Ragnhild. The old lame servant who came in from the kitchen poured out his tea in silence, and pushed it towards him with a face in which he read his doom. The Provst was wandering restlessly up and down the chestnut avenue. Heavy clouds of tobacco rose rapidly from his pipe, and lost themselves among the trees, showing more plainly than words, his state of mind. Provst Tönnesen only puffed like that under great mental excitement. Miss Ragnhild had merely told him at breakfast about the curate's appearance at the Meeting House; but in the early morning, while he was still in his room, which adjoined the kitchen, he had caught scraps of conversation between the cook and a rag-dealer who was imparting the whole story, so that his daughter's communication only confirmed what he already suspected.

A person now approached him from the end of the avenue, in a light over-coat, and a hard straw hat with a violet ribbon. It was Johansen, the assistant teacher. When the Provst caught sight of him he called out impatiently:

"Well, what's in the wind now?"

Johansen bared his curly head, stopped a few paces off, bowed, and said:

"Excuse me, your reverence, I have a birth to register."

"Oh! is that all! why should that make you creep along as if a misfortune had happened? ...

Whose child is it?"

"Netté Andersen's."

"Another unmarried woman! ... Of course, looseness and licentiousness on every side! Emancipation from every tie, that is the watchword of the times."

Johansen looked downwards and sideways uneasily. He was not quite sure to whom these words alluded; and his own conscience was somewhat burdened in this respect just at present.

"I hope," continued the Provst severely, "that you, Mr Johansen, bring up the school-children strictly in the paths of virtue. It is more necessary now than ever before, when licentiousness is preached in the market-place. Look over nothing. The imps must be tamed."

"I think I may assure your reverence that I have used my best endeavours in this respect. *I* have always tried to sharpen the children's sense of duty. But — h'm — it's good example which is everything here. Unfortunately, bad example has such a powerful effect."

"Yes, of course," answered the Provst, slightly astonished, and looking closely at him. "What are you thinking of? Do you allude to any one in particular as setting a bad example to the congregation?"

"Heaven forbid, your reverence, it was not my intention to charge any one in particular. I only meant — speaking generally."

"Rubbish! Don't beat about the bush — explain yourself properly. Whom do you consider to be a damaging element among the congregation? Well, speak out!"

"Hem! your reverence misunderstands me. I only meant — quite loosely."

"I say again, no roundabout phrases! Answer my question!"

"I assure your reverence it was only my intention to — to — that, for example, a man in the curate's position ought, perhaps, to be rather more careful in his behaviour, for the sake of the people. In the country, things are so easily misunderstood."

"The curate!" burst out the Provst, wrinkling his forehead and staring at Mr Johansen from head to foot. "How on earth can it occur to you to mention Mr Hansted in this connexion? I suppose you don't intend to accuse him of impropriety; well, speak out, man, and explain yourself!" he thundered, stamping his foot. Mr Johansen wriggled like an imprisoned worm. It certainly had been his plan to turn aside attention from his own irregularities, by making use of the peep into the curate's private life which he had had the night before. But he had only meant to raise a slight suspicion in the Provst's mind, without appearing as an actual accuser.

Now he was caught in his own toils, and saw that it would be best to give away Mr Hansted, and surrender at discretion. He straightened himself up, bent his neck forward a little, as if silencing his last scruples, and said —

"Well, I maintain — that is, — I think it can't be a good example for the people to meet Mr Hansted late in the evening, in a solitary place, handling one of the young girls of the neighbourhood in a very tender manner."

The Provst turned ashen grey. Again he measured the assistant master from head to foot, and said at last: "Who saw that?— Answer!"

"I saw it myself, your reverence!"

"You! ...and late in the evening, you say?"

"Between ten and eleven."

"And in an out-of-the-way place?"

"Out in Hammerbay, ...the place the people call 'the church.'"

"And you are quite sure you have not made a mistake in the slightest particular?"

Mr Johansen bowed his head and looked away in embarrassment.

"It was really not possible to make a mistake, your reverence!"

There was a moment's silence, then the Provst said:

"Can you tell me about what time — I mean what evening it was when you saw Mr Hansted in the said situation?"

"I can easily do that, as it was only last night."

"Yesterday! After the meeting! So then we have the explanation!" he exclaimed, not knowing that he was thinking aloud. Then he looked severely at the assistant teacher, and said:

"What you have told me, Mr Johansen, remains, for the present, between ourselves. Do you understand?"

Mr Johansen bowed.

"I shall look into the matter, and I tell you it will go hard with you if I find the slightest inaccuracy in what you have told me! ...The birth you spoke of shall be entered. Have you the papers with you? Very well! That is all for to-day."

When, shortly after, he entered the house from the verandah, he walked through the empty dining-room, threw open the kitchen door, and called out, in a voice which rang through the house:

"Are you there, Loné?"

"Yes," answered a muffled voice from the cellar.

"Go up to the curate and tell him I wish to speak to him. I shall be in my room. But say that he is to come at once. I am waiting."

Chapter Nine

The Provst was walking up and down the room with his hands behind him, when Emanuel knocked at his study door, and, without waiting for an answer, entered briskly.

"You want to speak to me, sir!"

The Provst did not answer, nor stop his walk, but waved him to a seat.

Emanuel sat down near the door. He held his head erect, crossed his legs, and put his right hand into the breast of his tightly buttoned up coat. His antagonistic bearing ill-concealed his internal agitation. Feverish red patches came and went on his pale cheeks with great rapidity; his eyes were dull and heavy, as after a sleepless night.

As the Provst kept up the silence which was only broken by his creaking boots, Emanuel at last exclaimed, in his nervous impatience, changing his position, and running his hand through his hair:

"I suppose you want to speak to me about my address at the Meeting House yesterday. I regret, of course, that I did not have an opportunity of informing you of my intention beforehand. I had meant to do so, but..."

He was stopped here by a lightning glance from the Provst, who had paused at last along by the window.

"We will discuss that affair later. That you have thought it suitable, in spite of the position you hold here, to appear as a wandering star in the weaver's troupe, I have already heard, and you will have to answer to me for so doing another time. In the meantime, there is a different matter, on which I require information. It has lately come to my knowledge," — he continued, slowly walking towards Emanuel with his hands behind him, and his eyes flashing; — "it has come to my knowledge, sir, that in one particular, where, more than in any other, you ought to set a worthy example to the youth of the neighbourhood, you have, by your conduct, absolutely scandalized the congregation. In short, is it true, Mr Hansted, that you have nightly meetings with certain young girls of the neighbourhood?"

Emanuel had risen. The feverish patches on his cheeks now spread over his forehead and temples, and his whole face flamed.

"Who says so?"

"That doesn't matter," shouted the Provst close to his face. "How does it stand? I want a short, plain answer, sir. So — yes or no?"

Emanuel bit his lips. It was only with the greatest difficulty that he prevented himself from hurling an insult at the Provst.

At last he said —

"If by certain young girls Anders Jörgen's daughter is meant — and there can be no talk of any other — yes, it is partly true."

"Oh, indeed! so you admit it?"

"Yes, I am engaged to her. No particular scandal can have been caused to the congregation, however, as it was only last night I spoke to her alone for the first time. And even then, as I now understand, it was not entirely without witnesses. Mr Johansen was also present."

The Provst fell back, first one, and then another lingering step. His hands dropped from his back to his sides, and hung loosely; he stared at the curate, as if it was on the tip of his tongue to ask if he was mad.

"What do you say? ...You are engaged to Anders Jörgen's daughter?"

"Yes."

In the space of half a minute the Provst's face went through a whole scale of the most opposite expressions. At last it settled into one of consternation mixed with the deepest pity.

Emanuel's face at this moment was not that of a happy, newly engaged man. His quivering features and heavy eyes betrayed, in spite of his efforts, the struggles of a mind distracted by the beginning of doubts and anxiety.

After a long silence the Provst came up close to him, and cautiously laid his hand upon his shoulder.

"Mr Hansted," he said in a low voice, "I must say a few words to you ...not as your superior, but as a true, fatherly friend. Perhaps, in your present frame of mind, you can hardly look upon me as such, and yet I assure you that is what I am, and I am only thinking of your good. No, no, you must not interrupt me. You must allow me to have my say. I must — do you hear? You don't know at present what you are doing. You are ill, you have been cajoled — seduced — I hardly know what. But I do beg you, with whatever influence I may have over you, to think better of this before it goes any further. Do you hear? you must, you shall! Good God! how can this have come about? Where has your sense been? What do you think your family, your friends, and your whole circle will say? Think better of it, Mr Hansted ...think what you are entering upon; do consider what you have at stake ——."

Emanuel drew back a step to free himself from the Provst's hand, and exclaimed —

"I can't allow you to talk like this, you are not in a position to judge of my conduct here, my joy, or my happiness, and it is useless to talk any more about it."

The Provst bit his lip, and stood a moment looking at him irresolutely. His broad chest heaved, his face was purple, he looked as if a torrent of violent words were choking him, then he turned away, and walked slowly to the window, where he remained looking out.

There was a dead silence in the room for more than two minutes.

It was broken by Emanuel, who said —

"Have you anything more to say to me, sir?"

The Provst turned.

"Yes, Mr Hansted!" he said with forced calm. "I feel it is my duty to warn you once more, most solemnly, against this portentous step you are about to take. I have received you into my house, and I cannot look on calmly and see you doing an injury to yourself and to others. Of course, I do not doubt that you are acting from the best possible motives," he continued, coming nearer. "Of course you are persuaded that this will be for your happiness, and for that of the young girl. But you are a dreamer, a romantic dreamer, Mr Hansted. I have long seen that! A craving for the fantastic is an unfortunate heritage in your blood, and it leads you like a blind man along unknown paths. Look at your true self. Tear the bandage of dreams from your eyes, and you will shudder at the abyss, to the edge of which you have been tempted. How has it happened that, with your talents and abilities, you have been blinded to this extent? What is one to believe, what is one to think of you, Mr Hansted?"

"I will not discuss that point. I only know that I cannot accommodate you by repenting of my actions — neither the one nor the other of them. When I spoke in Skibberup Meeting House, it was after having carefully weighed the matter, and I have no reason to wish it undone. I feel that yesterday, for the first time, the congregation and I were at one, — and if you, sir, had been present, you would certainly have been obliged to admit that the satisfaction was mutual."

"I am quite ready to believe that!" the Provst blazed out. "If you tell stories to children and peasants, and flatter them a little, they are soon pleased. If that is the grand discovery you have made, you have been a good while about it, I must say. I could have taught you that piece of wisdom some time ago."

"You make a mistake," answered Emanuel in a restrained voice, and with a dignified look. "It was neither tales nor flattery which opened the ears of the listeners, but solely the fact that I came forward as a man among men, not as a judge among sinners. My great discovery is this — if you really care to know it, — that a priest may have some other object than merely going about as the tax-collector of heaven, and keeping account of the sins of men — and on this point I received the most desirable confirmation yesterday."

"Oh, ho! so it has gone as far as that with you! You are already so case-hardened that I am to hear all the weaver's phrases from your mouth. Really you have been a willing pupil, Mr Hansted! If that is your attitude, I see that I may save myself the trouble of trying to bring you to your senses. ... But then, I suppose, you are prepared," he continued, raising his voice and coming up close to Emanuel — "I suppose you are also prepared for the steps which I propose to take after this? In short, Mr Hansted! you must choose now — either me or the weaver!"

"In that case ...the choice is made."

"Indeed! Very good! You talk very boldly! ...But — do you quite understand what it means? Do you see that your time here with me is over ...irrevocably past, do you understand?"

"I had thought of that. But from this time I have my own work to do in the parish, — and that, quite regardless of whether I am your curate or not."

"There now! It is a prepared attack! A downright declaration of war! You propose an actual fight among my congregation!"

"Oh, not at all! For my part I wish for nothing but to be allowed to go my own way in peace, and do what good I can to others and to myself."

"But not I! We do not play so lightly as that here. I am not going to be led by the nose like that — don't imagine it. It will be a trial of strength, good folks — and you had better not be too sure of the issue! Yes, you may look at me! Measure yourself with me, young gentleman! It might even yet put a little sense into you. Old trees don't fall at the first blow of the axe, — but that sometimes happens to the young; and that you will feel! You spoke yesterday, Mr Hansted! To-day it is my turn!"

Chapter Ten

When the Provst threw open the drawing-room door a few minutes later, Miss Ragnhild was just coming in from the dining-room with a large china bowl full of yellow flowers in her hands.

She was dressed in a loose morning gown of broad striped stuff with a cord round the waist, long ends, and tassels. On her head she had a flat, soft, grey felt hat, the only trimming on which was a white veil hanging down her back. She was pale, as usual, but the flowers threw a rich glow over the lower part of her face, as if it was a bowl of sunshine she carried.

"Whatever has happened?" she asked, alarmed at the sight of her father's heated appearance, and stopping by the heavy mahogany table in the middle of the room.

"You may well ask that! Upon my word I think the world is out of joint just now! People are bewitched — quite mad."

"But what on earth is the matter?"

"Oh, it's nothing more nor less than that our friend, Mr Hansted, has gone and engaged himself!"

Miss Ragnhild put the bowl hurriedly down, spilling some of the water over the illustrated books.

"What do you say? ... Mr Hansted!"

"Yes, as I stand here. But you will never guess who is the chosen one, Ragnhild!"

"Is it — is it a lady from these parts?"

"She is from these parts certainly; but she can hardly be called a lady. It is Anders Jörgen's daughter from Skibberup. What do you think of that?"

"Good heavens! is it possible!"

"You may well say so!" shouted the Provst — who, as usual, was walking up and down the floor with noisy steps. "Really, one does not know what to think of the mad times we live in. It's just as if all common sense was going out of the world. On all sides we have this bowing down to the common people, ...this worship of the peasant, it seems to be in the air in these days, like any other plague. How in the world are we otherwise to explain the fact — that people who up to this time have been ordinarily sensible, suddenly, and apparently without any reason, become absolutely possessed? Even people who were schoolfellows of my own, suddenly, in their old age, begin to play the fool, by dressing in homespun, speaking like peasants, and setting their daughters to milk the cows! And now this! It's stark lunacy! and you will see, Ragn-. hild, it won't stop here! This is only the first outcome of the folly. Others will follow. Mr Hansted has already to such an extent lost his sound sense and judgment, that, like all persons of limited views, who are absorbed by anything new, he imagines that he has a mission to fulfil here. He is to be the prophet of the new times, to found parties and lead riots, according to the fashion of these days."

Miss Ragnhild had taken off her hat and gone to the window with the mechanical movements of a sleep-walker. She sat down as if overcome with fatigue, and stared out into the courtyard. As soon as she saw that her father had stopped in a corner of the room and was observing her, she leant back in her chair, and said, without really meaning it —

"Well, in a way it's only what one might have expected from the turn which Mr Hansted's development had taken lately. One has long been able to see that it would turn to something of this sort."

"That is exactly why I can't help blaming myself in a measure, Ragnhild. I ought to have kept a tighter hand over him from the beginning. Who knows — perhaps he might have been saved then. I did at first have my suspicions ...but after all, he was a man, and you can't treat a man as an invalid, before you are sure of the disease. But now I haven't a doubt — he is mad — completely off his head! When I look back I can follow the development of the disease, step by step, from the day he entered our house. It is the mother's insanity coming out in the son. Once in her youth, I believe, she caused a perfect scandal at a public meeting, by making a most revolutionary speech. And — oddly enough — I heard, among other things about her from Pastor Petersen, that it was in these parts that she tried to carry out her wild ideas at one time. She was in fact the originator of the High School at Sandinge, to which we owe all our disturbances. In that case, one can say with truth, that Mr Hansted is a sacrifice to his mother's youthful follies. But that's the way of the world!"

Miss Ragnhild no longer heard her father's words, and she hardly noticed when he left the room and shut himself into his study.

She couldn't understand why this engagement made such an impression upon her. She felt there was no disappointment to her in it. In fact, her interest in Mr Hansted had been on the wane latterly; and it did not raise him in her estimation to find that he had engaged himself to a peasant girl. She thought there was something so pitiable in this ruling propensity for all that was undeveloped, petty, child-like, simple.

At the same time, she felt as if by this event, one more light had been put out in her existence; as if there was one more vacant spot in her heart. She felt that she had lost a friend — who, in a way, was her only one. But — what was worse — she had lost a sympathetic fellow-sufferer — in this wilderness of solitude and melancholy... Was it more?

She looked at her old friend Methuselah the parrot — he was swinging in his ring and pluming his green feathers. Well! she and her parrot were alone again! But for that matter she could imagine worse company, and she was not likely to envy the curate's new friends.

She was just stretching out her hand to caress the bird, when she heard footsteps creaking in the passage. There was no doubt about it — it was the curate coming downstairs from his room.

She sat still for a moment, her eyes fixed on her lap, in violent conflict with herself. Then she got up, walked across the floor quickly and opened the door. Emanuel was there with his hat on and his umbrella in his hand, just about to go out. He turned very red when he saw her, and a defiant expression came into his eye. It looked as if he was arming himself against her expected jibes, and was preparing to pay her back. She put out her hand in a friendly way towards him.

"Father has told me your news, Mr Hansted. I congratulate you most heartily!"

He looked doubtingly at her.

"I do not know the young girl personally," she continued calmly. "But I remember several times having heard most favourable remarks about her, so I do not doubt that it will be for your happiness."

After these words, Emanuel — perhaps somewhat hesitatingly — took her soft, white hand, and when she let him keep it, pressed it warmly.

"Thanks, a thousand thanks, Miss Ragnhild," he said, moved with pleasure and surprise. "You do not know how glad I am that you of all people understand me!"

"Well, I have perhaps had more opportunities of doing so than most people."

"You have — you have, Miss Ragnhild!"

"I mean — we have discussed every subject under the sun. Therefore you know that we hold different opinions on many points. But I hope you believe that I always respect people who have the courage of their opinions."

"I am afraid I do you little honour as a pupil, Miss Ragnhild!"

"Well! I cannot flatter myself with that — I suppose you are going to see your *fiancée* now?" she asked hurriedly.

"Yes."

"Then greet her from me, and give her my warmest congratulations."

Chapter Eleven

HANSINE had not closed her eyes all night either. She had come home in the evening in a half desperate state; her parents were fortunately in bed, so she was able to creep into her room and undress without being seen by anybody. Here she lay hour after hour, huddled up in bed with the corner of the sheet stuffed into her mouth, so that her despairing sobs should not be heard.

Although the idea that a young priest or a popular leader would sometime — like the prince in a fairy tale — cross her path, fall in love with her, and raise her, as his wife, far above the earthbound life of a peasant, to the summit of a higher intellectual life, was, as a matter of fact, no stranger to her, for it had been part of her dream-life ever since she as a school-girl had attended one of the big "Friends' Meetings" over at Sandinge; and although it was indeed true, as her friends insisted, that this hero of her dreams had in the course of the winter more and more assumed the shape of the curate — yet she had not for a moment, in the meeting with Emanuel, thought that his words meant more than an expression of sympathy, an attempt, in his position as priest, to comfort her and to reason with her. Therefore she now wished that she might die. All night she lay and trembled with apprehension at the coming day, because she could not imagine how she should ever have courage to look people in the face again, after having so ignominiously betrayed her secret.

All the same, when day dawned, and the sleepy chirping of the birds in the garden began to be heard outside her window, she grew calmer. She set herself more collectedly to go through what the curate had said, and how everything had happened.

The more vividly she recalled to her remembrance the occurrences of the evening, so much the more she was obliged to put constraint upon herself to drive away the thought that the curate had really asked her to be his wife. She remembered the tender tone in which he told her he loved her; she remembered how he had dried her wet cheeks and eyes with his handkerchief and begged her not to cry. And then he had also told her that he would come to-day to see her parents and ask for their consent.

She began to sob again. It was more and more impossible for her to explain away his wooing.

Whatever should she do? Oh! if only she had never walked home with Ane along the shore, this misfortune would perhaps never have happened!

At last she made up her mind to confide in her mother. As soon as she heard voices on the other side of the wall, where her parents had their room, she got up and dressed; carefully trying with the sponge to obliterate all trace of the night's struggles. In this she could not, however, have been very successful, for when she entered the kitchen where her mother was already busy lighting the stove, the latter immediately broke out with, "Good heavens, child! whatever is the matter?"

At first Hansine would not say anything, and busied herself with taking down milk pans from the rack. But when her mother saw that her daughter's silence on this occasion had nothing to do with her usual taciturnity, she continued to press her, and ended by becoming almost angry, and took hold of her arm to force her to speak; then Hansine began with a dogged expression to tell her that the night before she had met the curate down by the shore, and that he — that he...

She could not get any further.

"Well, what then? do tell me, dear child!" said her mother.

"He — he asked me to marry him!" she at last burst out, and threw herself against the back of a chair, sobbing bitterly.

Her mother clasped her hands in dismay, and for a long time could not speak.

"That can never be true, Hansine," she said at last, almost in a whisper, as if it had been the confession of a crime.

As her daughter did not answer, but went on sobbing mutely, she continued — pale, and almost ready to cry herself: "Who ever heard tell of such an affair, Hansine! — If I could on'y make out how it had come about! Whoever would ha' thought that we should have such a bad job as that! — What will folks say about it! It's just fearful, Hansine!"

Just then Anders Jörgen clattered in from the yard with two tin pails, to fetch milk for the calves.

ELSE·
IS·
ASTONISHED·

"What's up here, good folks?" he called out in his hearty morning voice, holding his pails away from him with stiffened arms.

When at last he made out, from Else's stammering tale, what was the matter, he pulled a long face, too. The fact was, that he had once for all got into the habit of adopting his wife's views, but at bottom he was not quite clear what there was to cry about here. He would sooner have been inclined to look upon the affair as a happy dispensation of Providence, but he took good care not to express any opinion which had not first been approved by Else, because he had no particular faith in his own powers of judgment.

Now he stood there with his curious dead looking eyes, with the bluish-white pupils, staring irresolutely backwards and forwards from mother to daughter. When neither of them said anything, he at last let fall:

"Well, but — well — however in all the world has this here come about, Hansine?"

"I don't know," Hansine answered at last half-angry.

She still rested her head on her arm, but she had left off crying. The combined lamentations of her parents began to wound her.

But now her mother went up to her, and cautiously laying her hand on her shoulder, said: "Well, but tell me, Hansine, d'ye care for him too?"

At first she did not answer, but when her mother repeated the question, at the same time letting her hand rest caressingly — as it were, forgivingly — on her head, she muttered: "I suppose I do."

"Because that's the root o' the matter, my child, that you both think it'll be for your happiness. For although it's very hard for anyone else to understand, yet — now it's come to this — there's nothing more to be said than to pray that the Lord may send a blessing."

"Send a blessing," echoed her father eagerly, his face lighting up with a smile.

"Now, if on'y folks won't be ill-natured about it, that's what I mind most," said Else, as she wiped away a tear with her apron. "There'll be enough spiteful gossip, never fear, and may be some will be ready to say right out, that we took up all this business about the curate on'y to entice him here. But we mustn't bother our heads about that."

"Oh, they can't have so much to gossip about," Anders ventured carefully. "I should think folks knew the curate well enough by now."

Else was never in the habit of listening to what he said, nor did she now pay much attention to his speech, but silently looked at her daughter in thoughtful perplexity.

After a time she said, half shyly, "Well, then, may be he — your — I mean the curate, will come here to-day."

"He said he would come this morning," muttered Hansine as before, without lifting her head.

"Well, then, we must get to work, we must tidy up the place against his coming. We wouldn't want him to think he wasn't welcome. You, Anders, must smarten yourself up a bit — when you've fed the beasts."

"Me!" said he astonished, as he looked down at his patched, grey homespun garments, where bits of straw and chaft were sticking into the rough nap.

It was a busy morning. As it was Monday, they had much of the unperformed work of the previous day of rest on hand. There was the cream ready for churning, a pan of whey to curdle for cheese, and half a pig to salt down. Besides that, there were the clothes to put out to bleach, and a sick cow in the byre to be milked every alternate hour.

Else, who knew she could not expect much help from Hansine to-day, and could not find it in her heart to make any demands on her thoughts, sent a message to a farm labourer's wife to come and help her. She soon obeyed the summons, but when it came to the point, Else could not bring herself to impart the news to her, although the woman several times tried to ferret it out, and at last asked openly if they expected company at the house.

"Yes, perhaps some one's coming," said Else evasively, and went down to the salting cellar.

In the meantime Hansine had hunted up her brother Ole from the stable and asked him, as soon as he had a chance, to run to the wood to Ane and tell her that she must come over at once; Hansine wanted to talk to her that very morning. Ole, who was quite in the dark as to the morning's hurry scurry, promised none the less to carry his sister's message to the right quarter, and a minute later she saw him speeding over the hills.

While she waited restlessly for her friend, she sat down by her chamber window to be undisturbed. She gazed out with her tear-stained eyes at the shady little garden where the egg-shaped spots of sunlight glided slowly over the grass plot and paths in their snail-like passage from west to east — and she could not understand how the world could go on in its usual way as if nothing had happened. There were the hens walking about quietly, and scratching up the earth under the gooseberry bushes; and the magpies were flying about from tree-top to treetop, chattering with all their might, just the same as yesterday. Behind the dyke she could see the back of the old brown mare shining in the sun, as it stood immoveable, letting itself be baked through; and she thought how well off was an animal like that. It had no sorrows, no fears, it knew nothing of this terrible oppression which made the heart beat till the whole body ached.

ANE·&·
HANSINE·

At last her friend came. With much shy beating about the bush, and many struggles with her tears, Hansine, sitting on the edge of the bed, confided to her all that had happened in the evening, at the same time taking a solemn promise from her that she would never divulge to any of her friends how it had come about.

Ane was not nearly so much astonished as Hansine had expected. She embraced her in an outburst of rapture and pride, but declared intrepidly that it was no more than she had long expected. The fact was, that she had had a dream one night in which she saw Hansine in wedding clothes dancing with a man who was exactly like the curate. For the rest, she added, it would not be such an unheard-of thing in the future, now that equality and fraternity were preached everywhere; so, for that matter, Hansine need not trouble herself. But it was not so easy to set Hansine's scruples to rest. Even when her friend, to cheer her, encircled her waist with her arms, and set herself to call up pictures of the brilliant future which awaited her, she continued abstracted and

98

restless; the time was moreover approaching when the curate might be expected.

"I think I must go into the parlour now," she said at last, and got up. — "But you must go with me," she added, putting out her hand with such a dejected countenance that Ane burst into fits of laughter. "Upon my soul, I think that curate has half scared the heart out of you, my chick-a-biddy! I don't know you again. Are you the same girl who never winced when one used to stick darning needles into you?"

"It's easy enough for you to talk," said Hansine with a sigh.

For nearly an hour after that, the friends sat in the parlour, both on one chair, with their arms round each other's waists.

Ane continued to paint glowing pictures of the future. Hansine tried to smile now and then, when her friend's fancy took the wildest flights; but she mostly sat buried in thought, and started nervously at every sound in the yard.

"I suppose we shall have to call you 'Miss' now," bantered Ane — "Miss Hansine Andersen — it sounds ever so grand!"

"Oh, be quiet, do!"

"It's all very well for you to talk like that, now you are going to be a clergyman's wife, but what is to become of us other poor creatures? I don't suppose I shall have a curate coming to court me, I shall have to put up with some old parish clerk, or shoemaker, or..."

Suddenly they both started up. They heard the sound of boots on the stone steps, and then in the outer room. In an instant they were off the chair.

Chapter Twelve

When Emanuel came in, his expression immediately betrayed his deep disappointment at finding the red-haired friend at Hansine's side at this moment. But he quickly controlled himself, and when Ane stepped forward and congratulated him with a flaming face — her freckles standing out white — he thanked her with a hearty smile.

Then he went up to Hansine, who stood half dazed, looking at the ground, and stretched out both his hands to her. She gave him — very slowly — both hers, which he pressed long and tenderly, while he gazed at her in silence. She perfectly well understood that he wanted her to look up, but she could not bring herself to it. When he at last released her hands, she stole a glance at her friend, with a sigh of relief, — she had been afraid that he would kiss her. At this moment the kitchen door was softly opened and her mother came in, in a freshly ironed cotton apron and a tight little black cap. At the first moment she was so ill at ease that, in trying to hide it, her greeting to Emanuel, and her whole bearing towards him, had an air of suspicious reserve.

Emanuel took her hand and said that he hoped the reason of his visit was known to her, and that neither she nor her husband would be afraid to trust Hansine's future to him. If they were favourable to him, he added, he would for the first time in his life feel perfectly happy.

Else answered by passing her hand sympathetically over Hansine's hair and cheek; then, as she was not a good hand at keeping silence on any subject which she had at heart, she said, "It certainly never entered our heads that anything of this sort would happen — nor can I say but that it is very strange to us. It's struck us all of a heap; for, as the saying has it, 'Like plays best with like,' 'The children of equals are the best playmates,' and you know Hansine has only been brought up as a simple peasant girl. I don't suppose your Reverence's family expected a daughter-in-law of that sort. One doesn't want one's daughter to be looked down on where she goes. However, as it has once for all turned out so, there's nothing to be said against it, and we can only ask the Lord to send His blessing."

EMANUEL GASED· IN·HER· FACE·

KERCHSEN

There was a moment's silence.

This was broken by the entrance of Anders Jörgen in his dark holiday clothes and white stocking feet. He remained standing doubtfully by the door, and looked at Else as if he expected a sign from her. At last he crossed the floor awkwardly, and greeted the curate with "Good luck to ye, and God bless ye."

Emanuel pressed his hand silently.

"Won't the curate be pleased to take a seat," said Else.

While the others seated themselves round the room, Hansine and her friend on the end of the bench under the window, Emanuel took the armchair by the stove. He was hurt and almost angry. It seemed to him that he had a right to expect a more hearty reception.

Else began to talk of the weather, and the want of rain beginning to tell on the grass and the early seed, about all the sickness among the people, and about the new parish doctor at Kyndlose.

Emanuel only answered in monosyllables.

At last the conversation dropped altogether, and a painful silence ensued.

"I say, Anders," at length Else said to her husband, "the curate mebbe would like to see the cattle."

Anders Jörgen half rose, and his eyes brightened.

"Aye, perhaps your Reverence would like to see the beasts."

Emanuel said yes, and rising with alacrity, buttoned his coat. It almost looked as if he meant to leave them altogether.

But then Else became anxious. She went up to him and said, trying to smile in her old winning manner: "Well, now, we shall expect you to spend the day with us? you will put up with what we have to offer you. If we had known it sooner, we would have managed to have something better. And you must not be vexed if we were a little upset at hearing of this. We never could have expected Hansine to climb to the top of the tree and find a husband like you. But at bottom we're right glad, and thankful for what has happened, and you must not think otherwise. You'll stay with us to-day, now won't you?"

"Dear Else," said Emanuel, immediately softened, "I shall most certainly from to-day be glad to look upon this place as my home. I have long wished to do so — and, in a way, I have no longer any other."

"Well, then! you are most heartily welcome," said Else, all at once regaining her usual familiar tone and slapping his arm. "We've always liked you since the first time we saw you, sure and certain we have. But go out now with Anders and look about you a bit. There are no grand things to shew you, for this is only a poor peasant's farm you have come to, but you knew that beforehand, I expect."

"I knew at any rate that I was not seeking that kind of wealth about which you country people say: 'The fire devours it in a single night,'" answered Emanuel, smiling. Then he turned to Hansine, and added: "Won't you come out, too, and give a look at the stables?"

She did not understand the hint, blushed, and said, with a glance at her mother, that she would have to help in the kitchen.

"Well, well, then, till we meet again," said he, and nodded to her.

Chapter Thirteen

Anders Jörgen and Emanuel went to the stables first; they were newly built, and immediately opposite the ancient living house. There were two big red Wallachian horses, and a rough haired yearling; they all rattled their chains and whinnied into their mangers with the hollow, comfortable sound horses make when they are visited in their stables.

With sudden liveliness, which astonished Emanuel, Anders Jörgen began giving minute details of the age, character, and breed of the animals. With great pride he explained that "the lass there" — he meant the foal — was a direct descendant of "Starkodder II.," who had taken prizes three years running at Roeskildé Horse Show, and could hang more medals and marks of honour on its breast than many a prince.

Emanuel listened attentively to him, and looked with great interest at the various appliances in the stable and in the adjoining barns and threshing sheds. He examined the chaff-cutting and winnowing machines, and asked the use of various screws and cogwheels, and had himself initiated generally into the mysteries of agriculture, of which he had seen nothing since his childhood, when he used to visit an uncle in Jutland. When they entered the cow-byre his attention was caught at once by a bird's nest which was built close up under the rafters, among the cobwebs, and out of which a pair of swallows flew just as they came in.

"Oh! look there!" he said with delight.

Anders Jörgen, who thought that such an enthusiastic exclamation could only refer to the condition of his cattle, let his hand fall heavily on the back of a fat beast, with a delighted smile, and said:

"There's a bit o' flesh for your Reverence!"

The cows were Anders Jörgen's pets, and he had a considerable reputation in the neighbourhood as a breeder and fattener of cattle. He knew exactly how much milk each of his cows had given, and their weights ever since they had been in his stable. He could tell off on his fingers how many pounds of bran, chaff, straw, and oilcake they had consumed; and the relative prices of butter, meat, and fodder for the last twenty years, — and he held forth on these subjects with a most surprising eloquence to Emanuel; giving him at the same time a most learned explanation of the modern stall and artificial feeding, and shewed himself a most determined adherent of the system.

Emanuel listened to him with rising astonishment. This little half-blind man, with his awkward manners — whom he had hitherto looked upon as a simple clown — now stood before him full of eagerness, asserting independent views, shewing insight, and unfolding a knowledge of his subject which quite overwhelmed him.

All this strengthened him in his opinion, that much of the want of appreciation, and injustice from which the peasants suffered, was entirely due to the want of understanding of the kernel which was hidden behind their external shyness and helplessness; and that therefore it was absolutely necessary, for anyone who wished to do anything among these people, to bind themselves to them heart and soul, to be able to win their confidence.

Anders Jörgen, who was flattered by Emanuel's interest in his occupations, became more and more communicative. He led him round all the outhouses and barns, shewed him the granary, the closed horse threshing machine, took him into the sheepfold, and down into the curing cellars, — and Emanuel followed him everywhere without opposition. When they arrived at the pigsties, and Anders Jörgen in his zeal wanted him to go inside to feel the pigs, he laid his hand on his shoulder and said smilingly: "Thank you, my dear fellow, I must ask you to leave that till another time."

At this point the white-haired lad Ole appeared, to say that dinner was ready. Emanuel nodded kindly to his future brother-in-law, and examined him closely for the first time. He was a fresh coloured, bright boy of fifteen, rather short, like Hansine, with a child-like expression.

"We two must make friends," said Emanuel, and pinched his apple cheek. The boy stared open-mouthed at him, and then at his father, and no sooner did Emanuel let him go than he ran away as hard as he could behind the barn into the brewhouse, where he told the woman, with a grin, what the curate had said to him. But the woman, who had made out what was in the wind, pursed up her mouth and said: "You're a reg-lar simpleton, Ole! can't ye see what's a-goin' on?"

Then he understood. He stared at the woman, his face blood red, and then turned round and ran away. When his mother shortly after stepped outside the door and called him to dinner, he did not answer, nor did he appear at the meal.

In the living room the table was spread with a clean white cloth and gay flowered earthenware dishes. The place at the head of the table was reserved for Emanuel. At first he tried to get Hansine to sit by him, but he soon discovered that it would be against all peasant etiquette for the daughter of the house to sit down while the guest dined. So he had to content himself with nodding to her as she carried the dishes in and out from the kitchen.

He was completely happy. The chill fogs of doubt which had closed around his spirit in the long sleepless night were long since dispersed. He was sure that his love would conquer fear and old prejudices, and it seemed to him that everything smiled and wished him joy.

The dinner was rather frugal to one of Emanuel's habits, and he did not know that rice-milk porridge followed by fried bacon, and scrambled eggs were looked upon as gala food in a peasant's house. All the same, no meal had ever seemed more festive to him than this. The sun threw its golden rays over the cloth, and he felt for the first time that he was indeed in the country. A fresh scent of hay came in through the open door, and first a white butterfly fluttered in on the warm breeze — like a little ship with sails set — then a busy humble bee, filling the room for a moment with its angry buzzing before it flew out again.

Last of all, the chickens flocked in, attracted by the clatter of spoons and forks; one by one they hopped in, as if accustomed to it, and picked up the crumbs off the earthen floor under the table and benches. Only the big strutting cock stayed outside, crowing softly like a wide-awake inspector, encouraging them and warning at the same time.

After dinner Hansine was so tired that she was obliged to go to her room to rest. It was a bitter disappointment to Emanuel, who had been longing to talk to her in private. He was obliged to be satisfied with Else for an hour, as

103

Anders Jörgen also saw his chance to creep away and take his mid-day snooze in the barn, with one of his wooden shoes for a pillow.

According to custom among peasants, Else took Emanuel all over the house. She shewed him the kitchen and brew-house — and here the smiling labourer's wife wished him joy, and offered him a dripping hand to shake — then she led him down to the salting cellar and the dairy, where she made up a pat of fresh-churned butter in his honour. Last of all, they went into the "best room," a big room with the walls distempered blue, which lay by itself on the other side of the entrance. The only furniture was a double wardrobe, and three large green painted chests containing their stores of bed and table linen and family relics. Else opened the chests one by one, and Emanuel saw many things which interested him very much. There were wedding skirts a

hundred years old, stom-achers cunningly embroidered in Hedebo stitch and with woven names and dates, which were the labour of years; there were ancient, gold-embroidered caps, and others sewn all over with beads, all of which had belonged to the wedding costumes of their ancestors; prayer books, shoe buckles, chains, and silver buttons.

Else was most taken up with shewing him the savings of years, in the shape of rolls of linen, bales of homespun and bundles of yarn; because this was — what Emanuel did not know, and never would have understood — the most important part of the children's portions, for the farm was leasehold for three lives, and Anders Jörgen's was the last.

"Yes, this is what we've gathered together," she said, not without pride, while she exhibited piece after piece of her treasure, passing her hand tenderly over them. "It's perhaps not so much, for Anders and I were married late in life, and for the first few years the takings were small. Then many a time we've had bad years, misfortunes with the beasts and the harvests, so we may be thankful we've done as well as we have. When I had my thoughts on Anders, my mother foretold both the poorhouse and all sorts of other miseries, but the Almighty willed it otherwise, and we've much to be thankful for."

Handling all these many stored-up things woke all kinds of old memories, and she told him how Anders and she had found each other in their youth while they served on farms together in a neighbouring parish. Emanuel listened, full of admiration, to her half-bashful story, how they had to serve fifteen years among strangers, and bear with all kinds of opposition, before they had saved enough between them to set up house, — and he felt a new joy in thinking that he might be a comfort and prop in their old age to this faithful pair.

Chapter Fourteen

IN the meantime rumours of the engagement, had spread from the Parsonage all over the district, and by mid-day it had reached Skibberup. At first the people did not put much faith in it, but when it was discovered that the curate had been seen to go into Anders Jörgen's house in the morning and had not come out again, they began to waver. In the course of the last hour the most diverse faces, both children's and those of grownup people, had been peeping over the garden wall and through the gate to pick up any scraps of information which could throw a light on the matter. While Else and Emanuel were in the best parlour, a pair of village wives ventured right into the brew-house, where they began a whispered conversation with the labourer's wife.

THE·DAY·
OF·THE·
ENGAGEMENT·

When by these means the rumour was confirmed, there was universal delight in the village. Nobody could now keep back, but all must needs press to the fence, so as if possible to catch a glimpse of the newly-affianced pair; and when Else and Emanuel returned to the living-room, they found a couple of intimate friends already seated there, waiting to offer their good wishes.

They were shortly followed by others, and it soon became apparent that Else's fears about gossip and jealousy were groundless. They all looked upon the event as a kind of honour shown to the whole congregation, nay, even to the whole peasant class; a living seal to the alliance formed the day before at the Meeting House.

Hansine, who came in from her room immediately after the first visitors arrived, did not by her manner give any cause for offence. Whilst her friend did not quit her side, but kept her arm shelteringly round Hansine's waist, with a triumphant expression, she herself shyly and shrinkingly received the congratulations of her friends in silence.

The room was crammed all the afternoon with proud and delighted villagers. After a time they were obliged to throw both doors and windows open to get a little fresh air into the stifling atmosphere. The coffee pot was kept boiling all the afternoon. Even Hansen the weaver appeared at last, and greeted the young couple with his distorted and ambiguous smile.

Emanuel was thrown into a curious state of mind at receiving the congratulations of all these people before he had had any real talk with Hansine, nay, before he had even had her consent from her own lips. He began to be almost jealous of that big red-haired friend who had planted herself there by her side like a guard, and who sat caressing Hansine's hand in her lap as if they were the two who were engaged. He was speculating all the time how he should manage to get Hansine out of this person's power and have her to himself.

At last he took an opportunity of getting near enough to ask her, without any of the others hearing, if they should not go and walk in the garden together.

She rose at once. But Ane followed. It was just as if she — Hansine's dearest friend — felt herself entitled to share their confidences. This time Emanuel had some difficulty in controlling his impatience, and after they had walked about for a few minutes, he proposed returning to the sitting-room.

But just as they were going in, he laid his hand on Hansine's arm and said:

"There is something I want to talk to you about, Hansine."

He saw that she trembled. This time she understood his hint. After a moment's hesitation she drew her hand out of her friend's arm and said:

"Will you go in and help mother with the coffee, I am coming directly."

Ane first looked at them in amazement, and then her face took an expression which was meant to show that she felt herself deeply wronged. Without a word, she turned away and left them. Hansine and Emanuel went slowly back the way they had come. Neither of them spoke. But when they reached the summer-house at the furthest end of the garden, where no one could see them except a little goldfinch piping among the foliage, he took both her hands and stood for a long time silently looking at her. She was pale, and once or twice looked up shyly and hurriedly at him. She waited for him to speak. But as he only continued to gaze at her with his tender, searching glance, she at last involuntarily crept into his arms and shut her eyes, while he pressed his first kiss on her forehead.

Book Four

Chapter One

When Villing opened his shop early in the morning, on the Sunday after the Meeting, he found the usual little group of ragged, miserable creatures, both men and women, at the foot of the steps, waiting impatiently, with empty bottles hidden under their coats and aprons, till the shop opened.

They slunk in past him, one by one, with a silent and timorous salute, and laid their greasy coins on the counter with shaking hands; meanwhile the shop-boy filled the bottles from the brandy cask, and then they crept out again, hurrying off— each taking his own road over the fields. Villing remained standing on the stone step in embroidered slippers, and a grey linen cap pressed down on his fat head. His thumbs, as usual, were stuck into the armholes of his waistcoat, while he drummed upon his chest with his fingers, and gave his morning glance round about the village. From his door he could overlook almost the whole village; he could smell what was boiling and frying on every stove, and decide at once whether the coffee beans or the spices were bought in his shop. Veilby only consisted of seven or eight farms and a few cottages. The farms were all built on one and the same pattern, of the same dull yellow brick, with a long row of tiresome windows looking towards the pond, the same high cement plinth and a slate roof. They had a small strip of garden either in front or at the side of each, with a few newly planted trees like broomsticks, giving neither shelter nor shade. The whole village had been destroyed by fire in a single night a few years ago. Only the church, the parsonage, and a few high lying cottages had been spared. Although it was only seven o'clock the sun was quite hot. There was not a cloud in the sky, and the slightest puff of wind raised a cloud of dust over the village and the adjoining fields. The grass on the dykes round the gardens, and especially the high hawthorn hedge round the parsonage, looked as if they had been white-washed; the surface of the water in the village pond was covered with an oily film, which glittered in the sun with all the colours of the rainbow. A man was polishing harness in one of the gateways; and by the gable of another farm, a man was brushing his Sunday clothes and whistling the while. The festive bustle of Sunday was to be seen on every side.

Villing was not to be taken in by this seeming carelessness. A strained and uneasy expression overspread his potatoe-like face with the little yellow whiskers; his outspread fingers drummed mournful tunes on his waistcoat, and he turned a troubled glance on the red roof of the Parsonage which shone majestically among the trees of the Park.

Oh, if he only knew what was to happen to-day! He would gladly give a hundred crowns to the poor for one peep into what he was pleased to call the "dim chaos of the future" — having a weakness for high sounding phrases. There was no longer any doubt that the Provst meant to use all his power to crush the spirit of revolt among the congregation — since he had nailed up an announcement on the smithy, that for the future he would preach in both churches himself, beginning with Skibberup today. But would he succeed? Had not the movement gone too far for opposition to have any effect? Notwithstanding that he was a firm adherent of the Provst, his spirits sank when ,he thought of the coming contest.

He went back again into the shop and vented his ill-humour, as usual, on the shop-boy, a thin bleached looking child from the Copenhagen slums, who had lately been entrusted to his care "by the direction of the Almighty," as Villing expressed it, and by which he meant an advertisement in the daily paper.

Little by little the customers dropped in, and up to church-time the shop was crammed. Most of them came, more to wile away a leisure hour than to deal. The shop was the common meeting place for the men, where they went at least once a day to hear the news, fetch the letters, and learn the day's prices.

The public mind was unusually depressed today. Rumours were afloat as to the preparations for war between the Provst and the people of Skibberup. One thing was certain, and that was, that the Provst had lodged a formal complaint with the Bishop about Emanuel, and had asked that he might be removed at once. Any one could see that the Skibberup people would not let this insult pass unnoticed.

According to some, the weaver had said with his malicious smile that there would not be peace in the parish till the Provst was driven out of Veilby Parsonage, — and what the weaver promised with a smile he usually performed.

Villing went about his business behind the counter with his ears pricked up to follow the various conversations. But neither he nor his wife — who had appeared in the shop like a sunbeam in a pink cotton gown — forgot to look after their business, and to take advantage of the number of customers.

Above the din of heavy boots, wooden shoes, and rough voices, Villing might be constantly heard giving orders to the bewildered shopboy: "Ludwig, a quid of tobacco for Hans Olsen — the best kind, finest quality! and half a pound of sugar candy! full measure, do you understand? no pinching for Hans Olsen, I beg" — or the soft persuasive voice of the mistress: "I think I may guarantee that you will not get the equal of this calico anywhere, at double the price. But the principle we go on is, when we have done a good bit of business ourselves, we give our customers the benefit of it."

Down by the door a man exclaimed: "Here comes the Provst."

The conversation stopped at once, and all turned to the windows.

A moment after, the Provst rolled by in an open carriage. He was alone on the broad seat, leaning complacently back in the carriage.

Chapter Two

By this time several hundred people had assembled outside the lonely church at Skibberup. Seldom — if ever — had the bass tones of the old bells pealed out over such a numerous gathering; never, in any case, over a more solemn one. There was as much stir in that solitary churchyard as in a market place. People were encamped on the gravestones; they shouted to each other across the graves, and on every side there was so much noise and talk, that the bells could hardly be heard.

The weaver wandered about in this excited assemblage, smiling quietly like a cat in a dairy. He felt that he commanded the situation to-day. In everyday life the people of Skibberup might grumble at his peculiar ways; but in times of trouble, they gathered round him with unshakeable faith — and hitherto he had led them from victory to victory. Rumour had for once spoken the truth, and to-day he was prepared for a master-stroke.

At the first moment, when the Provst's announcement made it plain that he meant to open the battle fully accoutred, there had been some difference of opinion as to how he was to be met. The young people wished to keep away from church entirely, as they had done before, and leave the Provst to rage to empty benches; and then, after the service, meet him on the road and hoot. But at a meeting it was decided to adopt a proposal of the weaver's, to muster in numbers at the service so as to have as many witnesses as possible against the Provst, should he — as was thought probable — overstep the bounds of propriety. It was now their intention to listen to him with perfect calm and attention. But if he went too far, they were all, at a given signal, to rise in a body and leave the church; and later to send a complaint, signed by all present, to the Diocesan Council.

On the stroke of nine, "Death's" bony figure was seen hurrying with long strides over the graves, from his look-out post in the corner of the churchyard. The Provst was in sight.

A moment later the bells clanged out again, and the women began to straggle into church in Indian file. The men, on the other hand, ranged themselves according to plan on each side of the entrance to receive the Provst without saluting him.

This was also done at the weaver's instigation. "For," said he, "it is nowhere written that people must take off their hats to the priest."

However, this little opening skirmish fell flat. The Provst walked from his carriage into the church without looking either to the right or to the left, and apparently did not notice the demonstration. Certainly one or two old peasants, when it came to the point, lost their courage; and there were a few others whose right hands involuntarily went halfway to their caps.

A few minutes later, before the men had all got inside the church, the hymns began, led by Johansen the assistant teacher. The singing did not sound badly, although the whole congregation sang at the tops of their voices. Whatever might be said of the dark old monkish church — and its musty cellar-like smell and mouldy arches had often been derided in the weaver's Meeting House — in any case it produced a softening effect on the rough voices of the singers.

After two hymns had been sung, Johansen withdrew to his high pew, and the Provst walked down from the altar and mounted the pulpit steps, which creaked under his weight.

At this moment a carriage was heard to stop at the gate; and just as the Provst began his prayer the church door was opened by an elderly man in black, carrying a white linen driving coat over his arm.

The sight of this person roused as much movement in the church as if the Almighty himself had appeared among them. Even the weaver, who had taken up his place against the middle pillar so that every one should see him, almost lost his self-command; his otherwise self-contained and clever little cat's face suddenly took an expression of open-mouthed astonishment.

At the first bench which the stranger approached, seven or eight men rose as stiff as statues to make way for him. But he motioned them to keep their seats with a friendly smile and a wave of the hand, and quietly sat down in the corner of the already crowded seat, next to a burly peasant.

The only person in the church who was unaware of the stranger's presence, or the stir created by his coming, was the Provst. At the end of the introductory prayer he took up his

book and read the text for the day. When he raised his voice there was a heavy thrilling under-current in it like distant thunder.

Johansen immediately discovered the commotion, and by craning his head over the pew he could just see the stranger, and the effect was to make his curls almost stand on end. He looked up at the Provst with a startled glance as if to warn him, but he continued calmly reading the Gospel, and when it was over he leant with both hands on the front of the pulpit and began to speak.

Chapter Three

EMANUEL at this same time was walking briskly, humming as he went along the path from Veilby common to Skibberup.

He had exchanged his inseparable umbrella for a more countrified oak staff, and in place of his former head-covering he now wore a broadbrimmed rush hat. The burning spring sun of the past week, when he had been constantly on foot, had tanned his face and covered it with freckles, and bleached his fair pointed beard, till it looked almost white against his reddened skin.

He had no clear idea of the stir that had been made in the parish during the week. As he was the object of it, the people — again by the weaver's advice — had not informed him of it; and as Hansine's parents for the same reason had kept out of the contest, he only knew that it was intended in some way or other to protest against his dismissal. He waited quietly for the Provst's formal notice, which must come soon, as he had been prohibited all clerical work. For the first few days after the rupture he had thought of breaking the last thread which bound him to the Parsonage, by leaving at once and taking some rooms which had been offered to him in Skibberup. But when he heard that the Provst had really lodged a complaint with the bishop, he decided to remain, so that it should not look as if he feared to face the responsibility for his actions in the right place.

But he passed as much time as possible in the house of Hansine's parents, avoiding any meeting with the Provst; besides which, he was filled with the joy of his young love, and of all the new world which was opened to him in Anders Jörgen's home, his fields, stables, and cattle, so that he only half took in what was going on around him.

At last he had his own plans for the future to busy himself with; and in these he often forgot the strife of the moment entirely.

He was quite determined to marry as soon as his circumstances in any way permitted. He thought of buying a small property in the neighbourhood, with what he had inherited from his mother, and intended to support himself entirely as a tiller of the earth. For the work he might do among the congregation, as priest or teacher, he would not take any pay. He wished to lead a perfectly independent life on his farm, sharing what he had with his friends.

He thought in a couple of years he might have acquired enough knowledge of farming — with Hansine at his side and the support of kind friends — to take upon himself, without any great risk, the management of so small a property as he had in his mind, for his means would not allow of more than ten or twelve acres of land, a horse, a couple of cows, and a few sheep.

He was already a pupil of Anders Jörgen, and had — as he thought — made great progress. He had learnt something of the manner of dealing with the earth, could almost drive a pair of horses, and could harness them either to a waggon or a plough, and knew how to feed cattle.

There was a little farm for sale beyond Skibberup — and he had already thought of it. It was a pretty little house with idyllic surroundings, at the bottom of a tiny green dale opening on the fiord. The buildings were small and dilapidated; to make up for this, there was an unusually large and pretty garden, with hollyhocks and honeysuckles covering the walls. One evening he spoke about the place to Hansine, who for the time was the only person to whom he had divulged his plans; and as she liked it too, and quite approved of his proposals, he almost made up his mind that this was to be their future home.

He had been every day since, to look at the place, and was more in love with it every time he saw it. When the setting sun threw a crimson light on to the small window panes and gilded the bushes in the garden, and the white wings of the pigeons as they fluttered backwards and forwards over the thatched roof, it seemed to him a little earthly paradise guarded by gentle angels of peace.

He already knew exactly how the house was to be arranged and furnished, how their housekeeping was to be carried on, and the labour of the day shared. First of all, luxury of every kind, and idleness, were to be banished from their home. The furniture was to be plain deal, painted red; and they were to live so simply, that not even the poorest person could feel too humble to take a place at their board. They would rise with the sun and the lark, and when the work was over in the evening, they would gather their friends around them to cheer each other with songs, reading, conversation and prayer. He already saw himself in a peasant's smock, following the plough up and down the ridges; saw himself rowing out into the fiord on fine evenings, setting lines and traps, while Hansine busied herself at home in the cottage, now and then coming to the door to look for him. How plainly he could see her upright little figure standing there under the eaves, her left hand resting on her hip, as was her habit — shading her eyes with her right, smiling her tender little smile so like her mother's, and which lighted up the stern lines of her face like a gleam of sunshine in a dark forest. Yes, his dreams carried him even further into the future. He saw their children running and playing on the sands, as happy as birds ... no pale, unhealthy creatures of culture in velvet blouses, with faces prematurely old; but strong, healthy angels of nature and the fresh air, with peasants' roses on their cheeks, and eyes as clear and blue as the blue waves.

He had reached the top of the ridge above Skibberup, and looked down on the almost deserted village, with its little orchards still covered with withering bloom. When he got a little way down the slope he caught sight of Hansine, in the meadow behind her father's house, feeding a lamb with milk from a bottle. She had on her cherry-coloured dress, which she had worn the first time he saw her properly, and in which he always thought she looked her prettiest. Her head was covered with a big white sun bonnet completely

113

hiding her face.

In a sudden fit of wild gaiety, which made him forget that it was church-time, he put his hands to his mouth and called "cuckoo!" She looked up hurriedly; and when she discovered him, let go both the lamb and the bottle and ran to meet him. At sight of this a little cold shiver ran through him, ...she did not run nicely. But when she came nearer, and he held her in his arms, he was almost angry with himself for noticing it, and pressed a kiss on her fresh, warm cheek. She had become fairly familiar with him by degrees, but still always blushed when he kissed her; and to hide her confusion began eagerly telling him all that had happened at home since the evening before — a sow had littered, a cow broken loose in the night, and the butter which wouldn't "come." Emanuel's new zest in his out-door life had awakened her own interest in all these everyday things; had, as it were, ennobled them and her home. He laid his hand on her arm, and so they wandered confidentially down towards the farm.

Else was at the window of her bedroom arranging her thick iron grey hair. Far from minding Emanuel's approach, she nodded to him, only drawing a towel she had round her shoulders closer together at the neck.

"Good morning, mother!" he said gaily. He had quickly accustomed himself to their natural simplicity of life; and in fact saw in it the simple leaning of the peasant's mind to the purity of childhood.

"How is all with you to-day?"

"Oh, very well — the big sow has littered."

"Yes, so I hear. How many pigs are there?"

"Twelve, I believe."

"Ah, that's something to be proud of! He looked about and added "Where's father? Has he gone to church?"

Else threw a stolen glance at him, and then looked at Hansine. "Have you told him anything?" her eyes asked.

Both Else and Hansine had known since the day before, what was to happen in church to-day; but they had decided not to tell Emanuel, because they had a feeling that he might not altogether approve of Hansen's measures, and also because Else did not wish that he should come between them and hinder their plans.

"Anders went down into the meadow to look after the young cattle," she said, calmed by Emanuel's look.

"Oh — I suppose we ought to be foddering now."

"I daresay he'll be back directly. But you're clever enough now, I expect, to feed them yourself, if you like."

"We must see about it," he said, and went across the yard to Ole's bedroom, which was next the stable, to change his clothes.

Hansine went slowly up the stone steps to the brew-house, loosening the strings of her sunbonnet as she went. She had to see after the dinner. She stopped on the top step and glanced uneasily over the little gate between the stables, down the church road.

114

"Not a creature to be seen yet," she said to her mother, while the only bitter feeling in her heart, namely, the righteous hatred of the Skibberup people towards the Provst, shone out of her beautiful dark blue eyes.

Emanuel went into the cow-byre dressed in a long belted sacking smock and pair of wooden shoes.

It was the first time he had fed the cattle by himself, and he felt rather nervous about it, but he weighed and measured out the portions with the greatest exactitude, and mixed the bran mashes, and, lastly, gave each cow a truss of barley straw.

His work soon made him warm, and he felt, after he had successfully accomplished it, that delightful sense of satisfaction which only bodily labour gives. Even after these few days of work he could feel his muscles developing and the blood coursing quicker through his veins. Why had he not long, long ago realized the old saying, "the sanctity of labour!" he asked himself daily.

His next labour was to clean out the cowbyre and wheel away the sweepings to the manure heap, the sweat streaming down his face. He felt the need of occupying himself with the hardest and dirtiest work he could find, to prove to himself that he had freed himself from the trammels of the past, and did not consider his hands too good for any work however lowly.

While occupied in this way he began to think of his family and the faces they would make if they could see him at this moment. He had had a letter from his father and sister the day before, on the occasion of his engagement; that is to say, he had received a curt acknowledgment of his "astounding announcement," nothing more. Hansine was not even mentioned, nor a single question asked about her.

Although he had never expected to be understood in that quarter, his father's coldness had surprised and saddened him. So they had drifted as far apart as this! He quite understood that they wished to shew by their silence, that from this time they looked upon him as past help and hopelessly lost; and that they did not wish in any way to be mixed up with his new connexions. He saw that they looked upon his engagement as a sort of social suicide, which was not less disgraceful to the respected Hansted family than his poor mother's had been. So he did not doubt that from this time his name would also be blotted out from the family recollection.

Chapter Four

When Emanuel shortly after stepped out to wash his hands at the pump in the yard, he saw a stout clerical-looking man climbing the steps to the entrance with the help of a stick.

When the man heard the clatter of wooden shoes on the flags, he turned round and stretched out both his hands towards him with a cry of joy.

He was dressed in a long-tailed coat, not free from spots, and black trousers bagging over his boots. Long shiny black hair hung in curls, reaching his coat collar under the brim of a dirty yellow straw hat, and his sallow fat face was surrounded by a reddish-brown goat's beard which hung down over a black vest buttoned up to the neck with two rows of horn buttons, so that not a vestige of linen was to be seen.

While Emanuel, who had no idea who this man might be, remained standing by the stable door, the stranger with great difficulty descended the steps; and though it was evident that every step gave him pain, he hurried across the yard with a beaming face till he reached Emanuel. Then he again stretched out his short fat arms and looked at him with delight, his youthful dancing brown eyes half buried in folds of fat, he exclaimed in a curiously soft, but penetrating voice: "If Mohammed won't come to the mountain, the mountain comes to Mohammed. For thou art Emanuel, — I need not ask thee. Thou won't find it easy to disown thy mother, dear friend! I wish thee joy!"

With these words he moved his brown stick from his right hand to his left, and grasped Emanuel's with a hearty grip, as if they were old friends.

Emanuel was quite bewildered. Who in the world could this be?

"To tell the truth, dear friend!" the other exclaimed. "We have waited long and anxiously for thee over there. Jetté has been saying nearly every day lately, 'I wonder if Emanuel will come to-day.' Oh, she is quite in love with thee already! When we heard of the grand meeting here on Sunday, and about thy speech, I can't tell thee how glad we were! And then, too, thou hast set thyself free and taken a bride from among the people! That's as it should be! yes, that's as it should be! But thou canst guess how surprised we were. Jetté wouldn't believe it at first, but afterwards she was so moved by it that it made her cry. I had to go over to the school to tell the girls the news. It made them half crazy, the hussies! They thought now there'd be a priest waiting for each of them! Ha, ha! Then we sang 'Love comes from God,' and then a lot of other songs, for when once they had begun they wouldn't stop. We didn't get to bed till after eleven. But we had the moon to light us in the schoolroom, the hussies."

At this moment it dawned upon Emanuel who this was. He must be the High School director from Sandinge. Now he recognised the face from a photograph which Hansine had. But he did not have a chance of assuring himself if he was right. The stranger continued to talk uninterruptedly, all the time patting him on the shoulder with his soft fat hand; then he took both his hands and squeezed them.

"Bravo! dear friend, bravo!" he went on. "We need all our young, fiery blood in the camp. We old fellows must get out of the way. Just look at me, I'm a perfect wreck. I am devastated by time, dear friend! Well, we old folks can comfort ourselves with the thought that we did not spare ourselves in our youth. And — God be praised — we have the satisfaction of seeing that our efforts have not been entirely in vain. Ah, you don't know how blessed it is to us old folks to see how the People's cause is winning its way, it is

116

spreading in every part of the country and among all sorts of people. And now you! Well, that's as it should be." This he went on repeating in the voice of a conqueror. "I couldn't keep quiet at home any longer; I said to Jetté this morning, I really must go to Skibberup to see how they are getting on over there. So here thou hast me."

"But won't you come into the house," Emanuel at last found an opportunity to say. He was quite abashed by the overflowing confidences of the other; and also at being found in his working clothes, in which no one had yet seen him.

"No, dear friend, not now — not now! But I am coming soon. I only peeped in to announce my arrival. I am on my way to see a sick woman, who's an old friend. Well, tell Else she may expect me to dinner, and I'll bring a few friends with me, and we'll sit and talk and have a good time. Good-bye, so long! I am glad to have seen them. Now I can tell Jetté about thee, she'll be delighted. I wanted to bring her to-day, but she had to stay at home at the school with the little girls. And we've just been to the king's city the other day, to the spring meeting of the "New Danish Community." Oh, they were beautiful days."

"But let us go into the house," urged Emanuel, this time more emphatically.

"No, no, drive me away, or I shall stand here jabbering till I lose my breath. Till we meet again, then! Good-bye, good-bye! Remember me to the family in there!"

He had hardly left the courtyard before Hansine appeared in the door of the brew-house, with her sleeves turned up and a bowl of scraps in her hand. She was just in time to see the broad back of the stranger disappear through the gate.

"I never!" she exclaimed, putting down the bowl on the flags and running to Emanuel. "Wasn't that our High School director. How was that? Have you two been standing here long? Mother and I were down in the cellar, so we didn't hear you. ... It was him, wasn't it?"

"Yes, I suppose so!"

She discovered the disappointment in his face by the tone of his voice, and became quite alarmed.

"Don't you like him? that can't be possible! ...You are never angry because he said 'thou' to you? He says that to everybody, even if he has never seen them before. And that is really right, you know; you have said so yourself...He is really so nice. You mustn't think anything else ... do you hear?" she ended quite pertinaciously. She looked so pretty with her anxious face and her sleeves turned up, that Emanuel, who knew her affection for her old teacher, couldn't find it in his heart to gainsay her, so he only answered by a smile and gently stroking her cheek. He was in reality not so much disappointed as astonished, confused, dazed by this ceaseless flow of conversation, the half of which he had not understood.

117

They had not, however, much time for explanations. Ole rushed into the yard, his face crimson and bathed in perspiration. In spite of his mother's prohibition he had not been able to keep away from church, and had run all the way back without stopping.

"The bishop has come," he shouted, as soon as he set foot in the yard.

"What do you say? ...the bishop!" cried Emanuel and Hansine both together.

"Yes, it's quite true. ... I have seen him myself. He came into the church when the Provst went into the pulpit, and now he's driven home to the Parsonage with him.

Emanuel changed colour.

"Then I must go," he said after a moment's reflection, and went to change his clothes at once.

When he came back, Else was in the yard, too, with Hansine, listening to Ole.

"Whatever can the bishop want!" she asked, turning an anxious face towards Emanuel.

"I don't know...we shall see," he answered, hastily taking his leave.

Hansine went with him, but neither of them spoke. She was white round her mouth and much upset. Altogether a strange sort of timidity had come over her since her engagement. It was just as though this event had disturbed something at the very foundations of her being; as if she no longer felt the earth steady beneath her. When they reached the hills she took leave of him saying:

"Then you'll come down this evening and tell us what has happened."

He smiled, full of emotion, when he saw how she struggled to hide her anxiety, kissed her on the brow, and said to soothe her:

"Don't be afraid, dear! why should any one wish to harm us?"

Chapter Five

The bishop's vehicle stood inside the Parsonage gate, it was a humble little gig, as like the veterinary's as one twin is like another.

It was in this carriage, which was the talk of the country, that the bishop, who was always his own charioteer, travelled about in his diocese, dressed in a white linen coat in summer, and in winter in a sheepskin coat, only accompanied by a young stable boy with a bright button on his cap. Without sparing either himself or his spavined horse, he journeyed in rain and sunshine for miles around the country, taking his clergy by surprise when they least expected him — very different from his right reverend colleagues, who always announced their arrival in the most solemn manner, at least a fortnight beforehand, so that everything might be ready for a fitting reception.

When Emanuel reached the Parsonage they were already at lunch — the table was spread, contrary to the usual custom, under the flowering horse chestnuts in the garden. This was by the bishop's desire; he said a meal in the open air was to him a most regal pleasure; so Miss Ragnhild — though not very willingly — had complied with his wish.

It had become almost unbearably hot. The glowing rays of the sun fell from a cloudless sky on to the glittering gravel paths with such a glare that it was quite painful to the eyes; all kinds of stinging insects disported themselves in the shade. The lawns and flower-beds, in spite of constant watering, were sadly burnt up by the sun. When now and again a faint breeze stirred the trees, the leaves rustled with a metallic sound like dead foliage. Not a bird was singing.

The spirits of the party seemed to be affected by the oppressive heat. Although the bishop was most amiable, and evidently exerted himself to set any suspicions at rest which might have been roused by his sudden appearance, both the Provst and Miss Ragnhild preserved a cold, reserved taciturnity. The bishop and the Provst had only exchanged indifferent remarks. During the drive from church, the former praised the singing and talked of the weather and the harvest. While the lunch was being prepared, he had looked at the garden with a great show of interest, and spoke of a new kind of English lawn seed, which was said to withstand the winter better than others, just as if his only object was to pay them a private visit.

From the moment the Provst met the bishop after the service he had been convinced that this man had come to take the part of his enemies. He looked upon his sudden arrival just at this point, as an attempt to humble him in the eyes of the congregation; and he had firmly decided to repulse this insult.

He did not dream that he had put himself in a very unpleasant position, with regard to his superior to-day, by the violence of his utterances in the pulpit. Only the bishop's presence had prevented the congregation from leaving the church in a body according to the weaver's plan. Moreover, it did not easily occur to him, that he might not be able to maintain his position even before the sternest judge.

The bishop was a little broad-shouldered man, with slanting eyebrows and thick hair touched with grey. He had formerly been in the National Liberal Ministry, and one of the late king's most trusted advisers. He was by no means without dignity, nay, his broad beardless face had at times a stern, Old Testament gravity. But his dignity was mixed in a curious manner with a whimsical carelessness, a remnant of the wild student temper of '48, which had been fostered by Frederick IV. at his court. This jovial unconstraint drew down upon him Miss Ragnhild's deepest displeasure. She always had a great dislike to any kind of democratic familiarity, and she was not at all impressed by the fact that it was an actual bishop and a late minister who threw himself back in his chair as if he had been at home, buried his hands in his pockets to rattle his keys, waved his knife about and called her "my dear." She entirely shared her father's opinion with regard to the bishop's official behaviour. She considered it most unsuitable for a man in his position to dash about the high roads like a butcher; and that his unexpected visits to schools and churches were unworthy kinds of espionage which must lower the clergy in the eyes of the laity.

But what more than all roused the enmity of the Provst against him was his position in public and political life, where his behaviour plainly showed that, notwithstanding his advancing years, he was still entirely governed by his ambition. It was also whispered that to get into power again he would not disdain the help of the democratic party, and that negotiations to this end were even now going on.

He spoke with great frankness to them himself of his weakness for politics and his love of power. They had hardly taken their seats at the table, before he turned the conversation to the rumours of his candidature for Parliament on the democratic side, which had just been going the round of the papers.

"Well, what is one to do?" he said smiling. "I believe it goes just as hard with old politicians as with old coachmen. When once you have sat on the box and held the reins, and perhaps used the whip at a pinch, then you can't bear to stay at home in the stable cutting chaff and polishing harness. There was a story I heard in my youth about an old coach-driver, who for thirty years had driven a diligence; when he grew old and had to give up his work, he could never sleep without a bit of rope or something between his fingers, and once nearly died when he was very infirm because it was not given to him. So I've often told my wife that if I am ever ill, she must make me believe that I have been named President of the Council, and then I shall soon get well."

When the bishop laughed, Tönnesen did not move a muscle, but looked as if he could not see the slightest occasion to join in his mirth. Just then, Emanuel appeared on the verandah, and came up with a bow.

The bishop received him, as a bishop needs must receive a young cleric, whose conduct has occasioned the sending in of a definite complaint. Still, his measured greeting seemed somewhat studied, and by no means served to soften the Provst. On the contrary, when the bishop, while Emanuel was taking his place at the table, continued his conversation and enlarged with a certain parliamentary complacency on the political situation, and took the opportunity of expressing his adherence to several of the movements of the "People's" party for re-arranging public life and its administration, Tönnesen could no longer maintain his passive bearing; he did not wish the curate to put his silence down to fear of the bishop.

"But it appears to me," he said, in a manner which was intended to overpower the bishop — "it really appears to me, that for the moment it is not so much that we feel the need of new movements and efforts, such as your grace seems to mean, as that we want quiet and decision, so that the different institutions of the country may regain their stability, which endured so many shocks at the founding of the new constitution."

120

"Oh, I am not afraid of a little airing!" cried the bishop with youthful gaiety. "Every house is all the better for a thorough cleaning from time to time; and I am sure it will do no harm to have the scrubbing brushes brought into play here ...isn't that what you call that sort of thing, my dear?" turning to Miss Ragnhild, who answered with incredible shortness, "Very possibly."

"I am, by no means, making myself an advocate for any kind of impurity," said the Provst with unshaken gravity, and in a tone of rebuff. "There's an old-fashioned proverb which says you must be careful not to throw the child out with the bath-water ...and in these days it might well be taken to heart. I honestly confess that I am, and all my life have been, a conservative, and I am utterly unable to bow down to these modern clean-sweeping principles. It can hardly be denied, that of late years many persons have started up in public life who will not be likely to do honour to their country. When education and accomplishments are no longer considered necessary for the public service, but are almost looked upon as evils; when every apprentice or serving-lad is to have just as much influence on the guidance of the state as men who have devoted their lives to the development of their intellectual powers, and widening their experience — such a people will soon decline, both intellectually and materially — there are plenty of examples in history for that."

The bishop, who had finished his lunch, was leaning back in his chair, with the tips of his fingers stuck into his waistcoat pockets. He had been observing the Provst narrowly while he spoke. He now crossed his arms, and with his head slightly on one side said, with an ironical little smile —

"What you say there, Provst, reminds me of a man who declines to use his left arm to work with, because the right has been designed by nature to do it — or has been used more — and is, therefore, stronger — he ties up his left arm so that it may not get in his way — till it dwindles away, and at last becomes quite useless. Such a proceeding — am I not right — would be looked upon as highly peculiar — not to say indefensible. Why, therefore, should the state not use both its right and its left side, even if the former — either because of natural or other causes — is, at present, the most developed? Would it not be reasonable if, in public life, we acted like a sensible man, who when he has a heavy burden to carry for a long distance moves it during the walk from one hand to the other. By so doing, you ensure yourself against exhaustion, and procure a uniform development of every part of the organism."

"Oh, I am sure there is no reason to fear any paralysis of the left side of the state," remarked Tönnesen. "It appears to me, on the contrary, that there is a good deal of left-handedness in our public life just now."

He liked this retort very much himself, and glanced at Emanuel.

"O yes — of course — I quite admit phenomena have appeared on the political horizon which are to be deplored; but such things can't be helped in stormy times like these. The chief thing is, by wise discretion and strict justice to conduct the lightning ...and in our days it is the most important duty of the leading politician. Nor must it be forgotten — with regard to the peasant class — that we have much old injustice to make up to them; and if perhaps, at the moment, there is a disposition to give too much prominence to the peasant, it is merely justice which has been too long deferred. We certainly need to cultivate new social strata for our spiritual nourishment, so as — if I may say so — to turn up fresh virgin soil, from which a Future, strong in vital power, may grow up. I am not at all afraid of the deep digging which is going on just now at our intellectual foundations. I have no doubt that it will bring forth good and sound fruit, when, by degrees, a sufficient admixture of the new and the old has been accomplished. Everyone who contributes to this end, appears to me to do a good deed, both to his fatherland and to his own spiritual development."

The Provst's face took the ashy-grey colour which was habitual to it when his blood was boiling.

These words of the bishop, spoken in the curate's presence, could only be regarded as a complete approbation — nay, glorification — of his actions.

"Oh, for my part, I have not the slightest confidence in this so-called 'Virgin soil,'" said he in a voice trembling with suppressed rage." It appears to me, on the contrary, to be merely sterile sand, or even worse constituents, which the glorification of the masses, by means of universal suffrage brings to the surface. If the madness goes on as it has begun, I am quite prepared one fine day to see our country entirely governed by the scum of the training colleges, and cowherds."

"Oh, those are only figures of speech! Should it really prove that the masses disappoint our expectations, or — to be more candid — that we have not yet found the right means to awaken the People's dormant powers, no irremediable harm will have been done. We shall at any rate have made — a necessary experiment."

"It seems to me that we have experimentalized enough under our new constitution. We paid dearly enough for our unhappy experiments in '64, with an accidental majority of the masses."

An icy blast seemed to pass over the bishop's face at this open allusion to the last unhappy war for which his ministry was by everyone mainly blamed. He did not change his position, but glanced once or twice uneasily at the Provst, as if he had not made up his mind how to answer the insult. Finally he put on his Old Testament mask and said, in a perfectly controlled voice:

"You seem, Provst, in your extraordinary want of confidence in the People, to forget the word of God which says: 'Thou hast hid these things from the wise and prudent, and hast revealed them unto babes.'"

The Provst wanted to interrupt, but the bishop would not allow it, and went on with rising voice: "In this connection it would also be worth while remembering that our Lord Jesus Christ, when he was on earth, did not choose helpers in his own work of salvation from among the learned, but — also in those days — from among the despised working classes whose life he shared. Ought this not to be an example for all time? Is it not time for us to acknowledge that our Saviour not only pointed out the way to realms above, but also, by breaking down the spiritual pride of the heathen, He laid the foundations of an earthly kingdom of righteousness, a sacred tribunal of the people, which it remains for those who come after to realize according to His great message, 'Love your neighbour as yourself!' The motto, 'Freedom, Equality, Fraternity,' which a certain newly-formed party have — unfortunately in a bad sense — adopted, that, in few words, is the whole teaching of Christ, which we would all do well to burn into our hearts."

Emanuel sat at the other end of the table, bent over his plate, following this conversation with lively sympathy. The depression which had followed on the bishop's cold reception at first, — because it was in such sharp contrast with his extraordinary kindness at his ordination, — quickly passed off when he heard him speak. His heart swelled as he listened to these words, which so clearly and exactly expressed his own thoughts, and strengthened him in the certainty that he now walked in his Master's footsteps, and was helping to create a kingdom of happiness which the Christian brotherhood would one day spread over the whole earth.

The Provst remained perfectly silent after the bishop's last words. He had eased his mind by his allusion to the bishop's unfortunate political past; and he would not lower himself by a discussion with a person, even a bishop, who, when in difficulties, could not avoid making political capital out of the Saviour of the world, nay, actually turning Him into a socialist.

Just then the warning sound of church bells was borne on the wind. It was time for the afternoon service.

The Provst rose and said in a slightly sarcastic tone: "Your lordship must excuse me; my clerical duties call me away. I hope to have the pleasure of seeing your lordship again when I return," - whereupon, without waiting for an answer, he pushed his chair aside and went away with majestic strides.

A moment after, the others rose too. The bishop shook hands both with Miss Ragnhild and Emanuel with a serious face, and said to the latter in a voice which was not affected by any recollection of the complaint:

"I should like to look about a little in the neighbourhood. Do you mind being my conductor, Mr Hansted, till the Provst returns? I daresay we shall find something or other to talk about."

Emanuel coloured and bowed.

Miss Ragnhild had remained standing by the table, her eyes blazing with contempt. She was dressed in a light summer dress with silk stripes and a straw hat with ostrich feathers, and looked extremely well.

When the bishop turned towards her to take leave, her face immediately changed to its usual indifferent expression; and when both gentlemen lifted their hats she bowed as stiffly as the most formal politeness demanded.

Chapter Six

The bishop and Emanuel went through the garden, and out into the fields by the little gate at the further end. The bishop lighted his cigar and threw open his coat, he blew thick clouds of smoke into the air like a man absorbed in his thoughts, now and then he made a passing remark about something which caught his eye.

Emanuel walked by his side in silence. He had seen at once that the bishop had a serious object in this walk, and he made up his mind to seize the opportunity and give him a full and clear explanation of his position and his relations with the congregation.

When they reached the top of the "Parsonage Hill," the bishop stopped and looked absently at the view; asking the names of some of the many churches whose towers shone like beacons in the hazy sunlight. He said a few words on the effect of the beauties of nature on the human mind, and the dreariness of a town life, and at last began to talk about the drought and the harvest prospects.

"I hear on all sides," he said abstractedly — "that serious anxiety is beginning to be felt. It would be sad if there were ground for these fears."

"I do not think there is, at least not immediately," remarked Emanuel, quite fluent on the subject. "The spring seed certainly has suffered a good deal, especially the six-rowed barley, and the grass land in hilly places is a good deal spoilt; but the rye is, so far, in very good condition, where it has not been touched by spring frosts."

The bishop turned towards him as if roused from his thoughts.

"Ah, ha! I see you are quite a farmer already!"

Emanuel blushed and his heart began to beat. Now it is coming, he thought.

But the bishop went on again, and again spoke of the difficulties in a town life and the influence of nature on the mind.

All at once he stopped and said, as if it had just occurred to him: "Tell me — are you not a son of Etatsraad Hansted?"

"Yes."

"Yes, I thought so," he added, and then said no more.

For several minutes the two men followed the little path in silence. A flock of hooded crows, which were startled by their footsteps from the ridges of a fallow field, wheeled about, screaming, over their heads; and not three hundred paces ahead of them in the path, a fox was slowly slinking along, stopping every yard or two to look at these two grave persons who did not seem to notice it.

"Mr Hansted," said the bishop suddenly without looking up, — "have you ever, in your student life — or possibly before — been specially attracted by any particular spiritual movement, either within the academic world or outside it?"

"I? ...No," said Emanuel slowly, looking up in surprise. "No, I can't say that I have. I have always lived a very solitary life, especially as a student. I have never, so to speak, taken any part in the regular student life."

"But among your comrades you must have friends who have influenced you...You have been a member of religious, literary or political clubs have you not?"

"No, and I have never had a real friend. I have been almost entirely thrown upon my own society and books since I have been grown up — I have never had anything to do with politics."

"Indeed," said the bishop shortly, and cleared his throat — there was a slightly disappointed tone in his voice.

"But however has it come about, then," he added, stopping and looking up at Emanuel. "How in the world have you arrived at your — if I may say so — somewhat extreme views? One's views of life are not got from books alone, even if these — as I admit they may — contribute largely to preparing the mind for personal influence, or help to form it...Of course," — he stopped suddenly and continued his walk — "I understand ...your home ...your mother were not without influence on your development. I remember you mentioned something of the kind to me when I prepared you for ordination. Yes, your mother was a remarkable woman, full of enthusiastic self-sacrifice and zeal. I knew her, as I daresay I told you before, very well in my youth; we belonged to the same set. I felt her death very much. She was one of those people who are too good for this world; and what broke her heart was the lack, at a decisive point in her life, of that power of resistance, or doggedness, which is so often wanting in noble and self-sacrificing spirits. I am talking in this open way to you, because I know that you are aware of all this; I remember you mentioned unhappiness at home as one of the reasons for wishing to take up clerical work in the country. Nor do I suppose that I am betraying any secret when I say it was — only after the continued entreaties, nay, perhaps even threats — and during a moment of feminine depression — that your mother gave way on the question of her marriage, which must have gone against her whole nature; and it was doubtless the feeling that she had been faithless to her ideal, which threw an ever-darkening shadow over her later life, and at last altogether extinguished the light of her soul. You may now be able to understand, my dear fellow, what a strange impression it made on me when I heard that you, her son, had taken up the threads she had been obliged to drop; and that you had begun to carry out in your life those views which, to her, were the most important feature of our times."

Emanuel did not speak, and kept his eyes on the ground. Lately, whenever his mother had been spoken of, and his thoughts were turned to her, he was so overcome by emotion that he could hardly help bursting into tears.

The bishop continued —

"But now, as an old friend of your mother — for I am not afraid to call myself that — let me give you some good advice, Mr Hansted. Or — tell me first what you are thinking of doing in the future, and about your position in this place. That you have chosen a bride here, I have heard from a private source; and I also know that, by your views and your relations to a certain limited part of the congregation, you have roused the Provst's anger against you. We have before us a conflict of a very serious nature. How have you thought of solving the difficulty?"

Emanuel confided his plans openly to the bishop, and told him about the little place by the shore which he thought of buying; and how he thought of living as an independent son of the soil, while he carried on his work as a teacher and priest among his friends.

The bishop listened attentively and looked at him once or twice hurriedly, and with astonishment, while he was talking. When Emanuel stopped he walked by him for a time in silence, and seemed to be weighing something.

Then he lifted his head and said —"All that you have told me is well thought out, and, in some ways, looked at from the right point of view ...but I must none the less dissuade you most strongly from such a step. I tell you honestly that I look upon it as folly, which sooner or later you will regret. If you take my advice you will not give up the ministry. The church in these days needs all young and strong energy such as yours, and what we have to do is to gather our forces together and not disperse them. Promise me, therefore, that you will put these ideas out of your head."

"My lord — I can not. I feel that I have my work to do here, and I am already bound to the place and the people with such strong ties that I cannot tear myself loose."

"Well — but who wants you to tear yourself away?"

Emanuel looked up in surprise.

"But — I thought — I thought your lordship knew that the Provst wishes for my removal, there is no other way open to me."

"Well, that is just what I want to talk to you about — but let us turn, the sun is too warm — what was I saying? Oh yes — what I am about to tell you is strictly private, an official secret in fact — which must on no account go any further. To make a long story short, the Provst will, in all probability, be sending in his resignation immediately."

"The Provst!" burst out Emanuel, stopping open-mouthed in the middle of the path.

"I said in all probability," continued the bishop, without seeming to notice the other's astonishment. "He has been offered — or is about to be offered — an important post outside ministerial work, a post which just suits his peculiar powers. I do not doubt that he will accept it, especially as his position here evidently does not satisfy him — has even perhaps become untenable. For this reason alone I should like you to remain. The living will thus be vacant, and you will be temporarily appointed to fill it; you will probably be left undisturbed for some time, as it is the intention to take this opportunity to make a long talked-of re-distribution of the parish. It may take a couple of years. I shall give no opinion on what the future prospect may be — for the income will of course be affected by the rearrangement; I. must leave that to

126

time and your own consideration. I shall not go further into the subject, there is no occasion for it, and I have perhaps said more than I have a right to say, but I was anxious to hinder you from taking any hasty step.

"I will only add, that in my opinion your work for the present is here, but I hope you will see that it is in your present position that a large and important sphere of work is opening out — certainly for several years. As I said before, we need all our young strength and power in the church ...

and not least in this very district, which has long had the reputation of being very backward in a spiritual sense — I believe even politicians call it one of their 'dead' points."

They had now reached the little gate leading into the Parsonage grounds. The bishop stopped and shook hands with Emanuel.

"We part here. Think it over, and in any case put off any decisive step for a week or so. Should you wish to speak to me during that time you know where to find me."

Hastily pressing Emanuel's hand, he hurried off through the garden.

Emanuel stared after him quite overwhelmed by his words. He had the look of a person who suddenly sees all his plans for the future demolished by an unexpected piece of good fortune and who just at first does not know whether to laugh or to cry.

·BOOK· ·FIVE·

Book Five

Chapter One

Five days had passed since the bishop's visit, but still the long hoped-for rain had not come. But a dry easterly gale had risen, which swept the fields, already baked as hard as stone; and for two days the district was enveloped in grey dust. In Vielby a catastrophe was hourly expected. They had arrived at the very end of the winter fodder, and the peasants, with their usual disposition to exaggerate, already talked of tearing down the thatch to keep life in the cattle. They had long given up consulting the barometer, or interpreting as omens the crowing of the cocks at midday, or the swarming of midges in the evening. Every morning the sun broke through the misty veil of night, pierced every cloud and drove away each shred of mist from wood or bog.

Then one morning the edge of the sky in the south-west turned blood-red and then pale yellow, dark yellow, and lastly blue-black ... a heavy thunder-cloud rose, a shapeless elephantine mass above the horizon. The people came out of their houses at the first subterranean rumbles. Even Jensen, the chairman of the Parish Council, who did not usually shew himself among the people, came out in his shirt sleeves, puffing at a cigar which was stuck into a wonderful carved amber mouthpiece. He observed the phenomenon of na-ture with indifferent superiority, his capital was disposed off in one of those safe concerns where there is neither ploughing nor reaping, and where you honestly make your four per cent, whether the Almighty sends rain or heat.

In spite of the sun, the lightning was plainly seen among the dark clouds which mounted higher and higher into the blue sky, while the sound of the thunder came nearer every minute. None the less, the Veilby peasants shook their heads. "That won't come to us; we'll get no good of it. "No, it'll go east-ward." "Skibberup'll get a splash." "Ay, like enough, they always get what they want."

Gradually a cloud came over the sun, and it seemed to shine through a red veil. Suddenly gusts of wind rushed over the hot fields; the cocks crowed, and the swallows skimmed hither and thither over the ponds in deadly fear. At last the thunder pealed just over the village, and the flashes of lightning fol-lowed each other quicker than could be counted. It could be heard to strike the earth round about. A sheep, which had broken loose from its tether, rushed into the village with a dead companion, tied by the leg, trailing after it in the dust. The sky was now one black cloud, and indoors it was so dark that one could hardly see the time. But not a drop of rain fell. There was a scorched, sulphurous smell everywhere, and as the air was not cooled by rain, it became so heated that every flash could be felt, almost burning the cheek. On the opposite shore of the Fiord a farm was seen to be in flames, and the piping of the fire-alarm could plainly be heard in the still air.

Just as the storm seemed to be blowing over, a few large, heavy drops of rain fell here and there, like stars on the dusty roads. The people began to come out of their houses, and were standing about on the steps, when heav-en and earth were shaken by a clap of thunder so violent, that several per-sons were thrown down from the shock. Simultaneously the rain broke out. It rattled against the windows like peas, and splashed the dust up on to the walls.

It was still raining in torrents in the middle of the next day, and the sky was just as black and heavy.

Towards evening Emanuel was sitting in the prow of a boat, in the middle of the Fiord, rowed by the carpenter. He was only protected by a thin great-coat and a horsecloth which he had thrown over his head. He was soaked to the skin, but he hardly noticed it; he was much too full of all he had seen in the last few days.

He was returning from Sandinge, where he had gone the morning after the bishop's visit, with the High School director. By this means he avoided all questioning about the bishop, by which he had been overwhelmed in Skibberup, and which he was not at liberty to answer. Besides, for his own sake, he required a little quiet to consider the bishop's proposals. The carpenter had accompanied him as a sort of adjutant, and the journey had become a kind of triumphal march.

Emanuel now understood what made the eyes of the young people shine every time the High School at Sandinge was mentioned. He was so taken with all he saw, that at times he almost thought it must have been a beautiful dream. The handsome red brick buildings covered with ivy and honeysuckle like an old castle; the great lecture hall built like an old Norse hall, with a panelled wooden ceiling with carved heads to the beams. The eighty fresh-coloured, young peasant girls, who were the present pupils; the singular teaching, which was conducted by means of lectures, reading, conversation, and singing; to say nothing of the evening meetings, when the people flocked in after their work was done, — labourers in their shirt sleeves — artizans in their blouses — he was enchanted with everything from the very first day.

He also understood the affection of the people for the Director, now that he had seen him in his element — in his school, where he hobbled about with his stick from teachers to pupils, encouraging, cheering, and admonishing all like a father. When he first saw him in the pulpit, too, the marvellous power of the man over the minds of the young became plainer than ever; he was so full of youthful enthusiasm, with such deep faith, and so carried away by his feelings, that the tears came into his brown eyes while he stood with out-stretched arms, as if in his love of mankind he would embrace the whole world.

The day after Emanuel's arrival there was a great meeting at the school, where he appeared as the principal speaker; and, by request, repeated his former discourse. On the following days he visited various circles of "Friends" in the neighbourhood, whither he was conducted by the director. He was everywhere received with delight, and made many new friends.

The visit also had a great influence on his decision for the future. He felt that the bishop was right, and that the little house he had thought of buying would not be at all the place in which to carry out such a scheme as was realized at Sandinge. He saw that large premises were required; many rooms, stables and coach-houses to accommodate visitors, and that Veilby Parsonage might have been built for just such a large, common parish home as he wished to establish.

So he made up his mind to follow the bishop's advice, and allow himself to be appointed to the living "ad interim," when the Provst left. But he began to feel anxious on this point. He thought the Provst would be quite capable of opposing the bishop, either out of spite or false pride.

He longed to talk to Hansine about the matter, and determined to break his promise of silence, with regard to her. His heart was so full of joy, and his head so full of plans, that he must have vent for them.

He had hoped to be in Skibberup before night fell, but at dusk they were only half way across the Fiord. The currents were against them, and though he and the carpenter took turns at the oars, they had great difficulty in driving the boat along. At last they each took an oar, and raising a lusty song, they both pulled with all their might, the rain pouring down in unceasing torrents all the time.

It was towards ten when they reached land, and so dark, that they could hardly find the narrow track between the hills which led from the little haven to Skibberup.

Emanuel took leave of his companion and hurried to the farm. A light was shining in the sitting-room, and no sooner did he set foot on the steps than the door flew open, and Hansine called out to him, "Do you know it?"

"What, dear?"

"The Provst is going away...it's in the paper to-day."

"Can it be true!"

A moment later, he stood in the room with the "People's News" of the district in his hand; and without noticing that the water from his soaking clothes was making a little sea round him on the floor, he read the following notice three times over: —

"According to reliable information, Provst Tönnesen, Rector of Veilby and Skibberup, has been appointed director of the newly-founded State Seminary at Soborg, near Copenhagen. The official announcement may be expected any day."

Chapter Two

ALTHOUGH the removal of the Provst was to be regarded as advancement — and he was far from giving any other view of it, rather speaking of his appointment with a certain complacency — yet the people of Skibberup looked upon it as a victory for their party. The weaver had kept his word — in a few weeks the Provst would be out of the Parsonage.

To tell the truth, the bishop had had to use all his diplomatic powers to carry out his wishes with regard to the Provst, who saw perfectly the real drift of the Pharisaic manoeuvre. But he saw equally, that, both for his own sake and his daughter's, he could not decline an offer which released them, apparently with honour, from a situation which had become burdensome to both of them. Besides, he was flattered by feeling that his past scholastic career was remembered, and his administrative talents appreciated; so it was with considerable satisfaction that he saw himself spoken of in the papers as the "distinguished Pedagogue."

In Skibberup they were very busy striking while the iron was hot. A deputation was at once sent to the bishop with an address, in which the hope was expressed that, "in filling the vacancy, regard would be paid to the wishes of the majority of the congregation." Emanuel was not mentioned, but the document was couched in such terms that it was impossible to misunderstand the meaning — namely, the appointment of the curate to the living. The bishop received the deputation, and especially its spokesman the weaver, very cordially. He touched upon the proposed re-distribution, which would necessitate a vacancy for some time, and further added that he always with pleasure tried to meet the justifiable wishes of the congregation. He then invited the deputation to lunch, and they spent nearly four hours with his lordship in the garden over their coffee.

A few days later the papers were able to state that the bishop had allowed himself to be nominated democratic candidate, at the forthcoming elections, for that part of the country to which Veilby and Skibberup belonged.

In the meantime Miss Ragnhild was waiting impatiently at the Parsonage for the day when she should leave it for ever. Although she felt too old to expect anything from the future, she had a burning desire to get away from the place where she had wasted her youth; and where there was not one spot or one person to regret. Even the sight of the curate had latterly been disagreeable to her, and had a most depressing effect upon her. It was not only that he had become careless in his person, or because his hair and his clothes smelt of the stable when he occasionally dined at the Parsonage. But she thought a corresponding change had taken place in his inner being, and that his original good breeding was disappearing in his efforts to acquire a broad "popular" manner.

Ever since his visit to Sandinge, she thought a certain smug self-importance had come over him. He had become clumsily ironical in speaking of her dress and her idle life; and she found his everlasting didactic lectures absolutely intolerable.

She was weary of existence, and daily more depressed by an infinite melancholy. By way of cheering herself, she had lately paid a visit to Copenhagen, where she had not been for two or three years. But melancholy followed her here too. She did not know whether it was the state of her own spirits at the moment, but it appeared to her that the everlasting peasant was celebrating his triumphs in every direction. The shop windows, with their tasteless cheap goods, seemed to be only designed to suit the taste of the common people. All distinguished taste seemed to be disappearing from the world; the current literature only dealt with peasants and work-people. The artists at the Charlottenburg exhibition all seemed enamoured of such subjects as "In a peasant's room;" "Pigs on a dunghill;" "A shoemaker at his last." Even in the theatres there was no immunity, for the peasant Members of Parliament had their free seats.

One day she met in the street a friend of her youth, whom she had not seen for ten years — she had married a doctor.

Before they had said ten words to each other, the friend, who was dressed like a scarecrow, began criticising her dress, and could talk of nothing but the cause of the people, in which she was determined to interest her. Ragnhild had no peace till she went with her to the house of a Mrs Gylling, who held a kind of "Popular Court" in the capital. She was obliged to sit for an hour in an assemblage of chattering High School people, peasants, and theological students, whose big beards reeked with tobacco. Several elderly ladies, who all wore velvet hoods of the same shape as those worn by the peasant women, surrounded her with offensive familiarity. An anaemic-looking young lady, with two long yellow plaits hanging down her back, was sitting in a dreamy attitude with her arms round a big dressed-up peasant girl, whom, in a languishing way, she called her "dearest friend."

What depressed her more than anything was the rumour of a possible change of ministry. It was seriously said that the peasants would come into power. A former village schoolmaster was pointed out as the future Prime Minister. Even people who could not reconcile themselves to the present state of things shook their heads and said, "there was nothing else to be done." She could not understand it at all. Had not the peasants always been in a majority? Why then this sudden subjection to them? "After all, the peasant is a man," was the answer always given to her objections. Now, that is just what they are not! Perhaps they were, according to natural history, reckoned by the number of their grinders, etc. But a country yokel was none the less, much more closely allied to his sheep or his cattle than to even an ordinarily intelligent person. Nobody thought of giving votes to sheep or cattle. Could it really be called justice to let everything great and beautiful be laid waste, merely because a certain number of individuals were created with the same number of grinding teeth as man? Oh, would not some man soon arise with the courage and the heart of a man to maintain his old lordship, and drive this peasant brood back to the dunghills where he belonged?

At last, in the middle of July, the Tönnesens were able to pack up their things and leave. The Veilby parishioners and three landowners had some idea of honouring the Provst with a farewell dinner and a silver coffee pot; but, at the instance of Miss Ragnhild, he found means to hinder the project.

The Provst parted from his congregation with only the most necessary formalities, but without any particular bitterness. He only disclosed the true state of his feelings to Emanuel, when on leaving, he coldly shook hands with him, and said that it was unnecessary to wish people good luck when they were fortunate enough to have the "Wind of the Times" in their sails.

As soon as they left, Emanuel moved down from his attic, with his few articles of furniture, and established himself in the Provst's study and one of the bedrooms. All the rest of the house was empty, except the room occupied by the old lame servant, who for the time remained as his housekeeper. No one had asked her to stay, but she seemed to take it for granted that she went with the house as one of the fixtures, and Emanuel good-naturedly agreed. "Maren" went with the Tönnesens, as well as the horses and carriages, and there was no need to get a new man; for, to Emanuel's great annoyance, the Parsonage glebe land was let to one of the peasants, whose lease would not expire for a year.

He passed all the time he could spare from his clerical duties at the farm at Skibberup, where he took part in all kinds of work daily. He ploughed, hoed turnips, and carted manure on to the fallow land. In the evening he would sit in the garden with Hansine, looking at the sunsets and talking of the future, or they walked hand in hand through the fields looking at the crops and the cattle. Now, when his way lay smoothly before him, he had more quiet to devote to his love, and he gave himself up to it with ever-increasing pleasure.

Chapter Three

IN this way the time passed happily till the autumn set in, with short, stormy days and long dark nights.

Then Emanuel found it every evening more difficult to take leave of Hansine, and the warm, cosy room at the farm; and to trudge home over the muddy roads to the empty Parsonage, where his steps echoed as in a vault. He always went straight to bed; but though he was tired with his work, he was often kept awake by the various indescribable sounds which haunt an empty house at night. Or else he lay awake listening to the wild moaning of wind through the trees in the garden, which sounded like great waves thundering one on the top of the other.

One night he was awakened by a long-drawn wailing sound, which at first he could not explain, until he made out that it was the piping of the fire alarm. He sprang up in haste and was hurrying on a few clothes, when he heard sounds in the house; the door opened, and the lame servant appeared in a flannel petticoat, with a lighted candle in her shaking hands.

"Oh, sir! ...There's a fire!" she screamed, with a pale face — like everyone else who had been through the great Veilby fire, she could never hear the fire alarm without being frightened to death.

People were running about all over the village with lanterns. It was soon discovered that it was only a cottage in the next parish which was on fire; and when the hose had been got off, sufficiently manned, the village settled down again.

This disturbance so upset Emanuel that he made a decided resolution the same night. He was determined to be married soon. He felt that he could not endure this dreary solitude during a long, dark winter. And why should he wait? - for the present, at all events, there would be no change in his position.

The very next day he spoke to Hansine about it.

At first she was a good deal alarmed. She had secretly hoped that Emanuel would not want to be married for a year at least. The more narrowly she examined her new position — especially after there was a prospect of becoming mistress of the palatial Veilby Parsonage — so much the more she feared not doing justice to the position in which her marriage would place her. But when she saw how happy and sanguine Emanuel always was, and how anxious he was to hurry on the marriage, she could not find it in her heart to oppose his wishes, or even to disturb him with her troubles; and when her parents were consulted, it was decided at a family council that the wedding should take place on the 6th of October, Frederick the VIIth's birthday.

But now a little difficulty arose, the outcome of which was anxiously looked for in the village. While Hansine wanted to be married as quietly as possible, her mother thought they owed it to Emanuel to celebrate the day with as much splendour as they could. Otherwise, he might still think they were not thoroughly pleased with the connection, and she wanted for once to shew her gratitude by her deeds.

Emanuel took no part in the arrangements, and, indeed, did not seem to notice them; personally, he did not object to a gathering of "Friends" on his wedding-day, but he did not wish to influence the decision of the others. So, for the first time in their three-and-twenty years of married life, it came about that Else and Anders did not agree. He saw that, if Else had her way, it would fall very heavily on his carefully hoarded little capital — a sum of six hundred kroner; it had always been destined for the purchase of a threshing machine, which he had wanted for ten years. He tried to get her to see how unreasonable it was, for the sake of a single day, to waste a sum which would serve to thresh their grain to the end of their days. Emanuel knew well enough, he said, how fond they were of him, and perhaps he would not care to see so much money thrown out of the window. Else was almost on the point of yielding when she received support from an unexpected quarter.

On Sunday afternoon, Villing and his wife paid a solemn visit of congratulation; the banns had been called for the first time that day, so it was now officially known. The lady was in a silk dress and crepe shawl, and her gentle, nun-like face wore a benignant smile; Villing was in a tall hat and frock coat, well-padded on the shoulders, a white waistcoat with glass buttons, and white cuffs coming well down over his swollen hands, which were encased in dog-skin gloves.

Since co-operative stores had been started in Skibberup, under the leadership of the weaver, they had not set foot in the place; but recent events had considerably softened their feelings. They now saw that they had judged the people harshly, and as it was against their nature to live at enmity with anyone, they took this opportunity of atoning for their injustice.

Only Else and Anders were present during the visit, and at first the conversation turned upon indifferent topics. But suddenly the shopkeeper asked about the approaching marriage, and then Else, with her usual frankness, told them of the difference which had arisen between herself and Anders as to the celebration.

Villing, who hitherto was sitting with rather an absent air nursing his tall hat on his knee started up at these words and became very conversational.

He must confess — he said — that he did not understand Anders Jörgen's attitude in this affair. It appeared to him that such an important event ought to be celebrated in a suitable manner; that it was a downright point of honour for Anders Jörgen's house to make the day a high festival for all friends of the "People's Cause." He knew, he added, that the whole neighbourhood were anxious to take this opportunity of shewing their friendly feelings to the young couple; and he was convinced that the participation of the people would give to the solemnity the character of a true National Festival.

While he talked, Anders Jörgen shrank up like a snail in its shell, and glanced anxiously at his wife. When Villing noticed that his words were having an effect, he continued to talk. It was quite evident that he had all the arrangements mapped out in his head.

His advice was to have a large tent pitched in the meadow behind the farmyard, where they could dine; and then he proposed to get leave to use the Meeting House for dancing, and decorate it. They need not be alarmed about the expenses; if they would do him the honour to put the whole affair in his hands, and trust him to make the necessary purchases, he would promise that it should not cost them more than a couple of hundred kr. He knew that for the last few years the people of Skibberup had withdrawn their custom from him; but he wished to take this opportunity of shewing them that they had mistaken him, that both he and his wife were their true and disinterested friends. These observations were seconded by Mrs Villing, who laid her hand on Else's arm and looked at her in the most affectionate manner.

The shopkeeper's persuasions at last overcame Anders Jörgen's scruples, and when Else had had another conversation with Hansine, she also fell in with her mother's plans.

Villing was really in the right. There was a growing desire throughout the neighbourhood to do honour to Emanuel, who by his gentle manners, his straightforwardness, and his constant anxiety to meet their wishes, had, by degrees, won over even the Veilby people, so that they crowded to church every Sunday too. Even a man like Jensen, the chairman of the Parish Council, made advances to him, and Aggerbölle the vet. had long since declared him to be a "devilish good preacher," and an excellent young man.

There was still one of the peasant fraternity who held aloof, and that was Maren Smeds, the hideous little woman who had taken such a prominent part on the occasion of Emanuel's first speech. Her history was as follows.

Having in her youth once been kitchen-maid in a gentleman's house, she was, for a long time, chosen to cook all the great feasts of the neighbourhood, a position which gained for her both glory and comfortable means. At a great christening feast, at which more than a hundred guests were present, she had the misfortune to burn the rice porridge. Although her husband, who was then alive and acting as master of the ceremonies, immediately thrashed her soundly before the eyes of all the company, the people would never have any more to do with her, and ever afterwards had their cooks from the town.

This was the cause of that hatred of her kind, which made the poor crea-ture the only socialist in the place; and since the affair in the Meeting House all her bitterness had been spent on Emanuel.

Hansine, who at this time was most anxious to conciliate every one, and in her timorous love, to disperse every threatening cloud from her future, one afternoon went to the tumble-down hut, a long way beyond the village, where Maren lived, to ask her to come and cook at her wedding. The poor creature was overwhelmed by the revulsion of feeling. After a moment's struggle with her pride she burst into loud and uncontrollable sobs, and — to Hansine's great discomfiture — fell on her knees and kissed her hand.

Chapter Four

The wedding day broke clear and calm, and nearly as hot as sum-mer. For more than a week, and all through the last night, baking and boiling had been going on at the Farm. The cellars were filled to overflowing with huge joints, mighty hams, brawn and smoked legs of mutton. There were tubs of sausages, baskets heaped with boiled eggs, and lump sugar, ox tongues and dried herrings, mounds of butter and prune tarts as big as cart wheels. These last sent, according to custom, as wedding gifts by the oldest friends of the family.

Neilsen the carpenter and a couple of assistants were putting the finishing touches to the big tent in the little meadow behind the house; while the young girls were busy decorating the walls of the Meeting House with gar-lands of fir and painted shields. Flags were flying all over the village, and two masts were raised in front of the bride's house, entwined with green, bearing between them a banner with the word "Welcome."

The marriage was to take place at twelve o'clock, but as early as ten the guests began to appear. Emanuel arrived early. After much consideration he had decided to be married in his robes.

Lunch tables were spread in the blue-washed "best room," where no less a person than Villing was acting as master of the ceremonies. In this character he received all the men and served "Snaps" and ale. Emanuel had specially desired that the marriage customs of the neighbourhood were in no way to be broken. He refused the "Snaps," however, and contented himself with a glass of ale. In the course of an hour the rooms were filled with gaily dressed people, and the great question among them was, — who would perform the ceremony? Emanuel had seen the bishop some time before on the subject, and he had hinted at the possibility of coming himself. As an old friend of Emanuel's mother, he said, he was, in a way, the most suitable person. They were all much excited now as to whether such an honour would be shewn to the congregation.

At half-past eleven the peasants' "Holstein waggons" came up, some thirty odd, and they began to take their seats. The carriages for the bridal pair and their nearest friends were drawn up in the courtyard; the others formed a line outside, reaching from the bride's house to the end of the village.

In the meantime Hansine was sitting in her room, because the guests might not see the bride till they were all seated in the carriages. Then she appeared on the stone steps at Emanuel's side. She wore a black woollen dress with narrow lace at the throat and wrists. Under the bridal veil and wreath of myrtle she had a closely fitting cap, thickly embroidered with gold and beads, which had been part of her great-grandmother's bridal costume. She wore it today by Emanuel's special wish. The lunch had loosened the

tongues of many of the men already, and there was plenty of gossip on the way to church. The buzz only died down when they came within sound of the bells, and Else began to cry. Hansine, on the contrary, kept the fixed and reserved expression which was usual to her in moments of strong emotion. The church, the haze, the blue shallows of the Fiord, and the opposite shore — all lay bathed in golden sunshine. Clouds of starlings skimmed along, and white gulls were screaming over the water.

On reaching the churchyard wall the bishop's gig was seen, and the bishop himself was standing in front of the church door in his silk gown and with his orders on his breast to receive them. It was a solemn and memorable moment for them all, when — uncovering his white head — he went to meet the bridal pair, and led the way into the church at the head of the procession.

The address was short and in the tone of an ordinary speech. The bishop belonged to those modern preachers who adopt an easy conversational voice, and pronounce such words as "Christ" and "The Holy Ghost" with the same simplicity as in naming a friend. His speech was a repetition of what he had said on a former occasion at the luncheon table at Veilby Parsonage; the same pictures and expressions occurred here again. He first compared Emanuel with a plant, seeking a new soil; then the congregation to a big tree, in whose shelter and shade the plant was to grow. He concluded by calling down a blessing from the Lord on the new covenant which was here sealed.

On the conclusion of the ceremony they all assembled in the churchyard, and the Bishop greeted several of the people, taking the opportunity to single out Hansen, the weaver. Else thanked the bishop with much emotion for the honour he had shown to her daughter and her son-in-law, and invited him to join the wedding festivities, but he excused himself, having to be home before evening. After changing his gown in the vestry for the linen driving coat, he again shook hands with the bridal pair and some of the bystanders, mounted his gig and drove off.

Immediately afterwards the bridal procession started homewards with much cracking of whips. Guns were fired from various farms and meadows as they drove through the village, amid rearing of horses and screaming of women.

Four musicians with violins and horns stood outside the bride's house, and struck up a tune every time a conveyance stopped to set down visitors. Some of these were stiff old grandfathers, and stout, heavy women, who had to be helped down by three men; the smiling young girls, with their floating red ribbons, sprang out into the arms of any youth who came forward.

All the "Friends," both from Skibberup itself and the surrounding country, had been invited, but most of the young folks were only to come to the dance. Even old Erik was limping about with his Sunday crutch, while, with a beaming face, he snuffed the savoury odours of roast meat which hung about the house, and filled both the courtyard and the garden.

The director of the High School, who had been becalmed on the Fiord, now arrived with his Jetté, a tall bony female with a red face and spectacles. He hobbled about among the guests with a broad, benignant smile; slapping the men on the shoulder, shaking hands with the women, making lively remarks, and slyly pinching the cheeks of the girls. The weaver, on the other hand, went about silently with his hands on his back, smiling ambiguously first on one side of his face and then on the other.

When all the guests were assembled, Villing appeared on the outer stone steps in white gloves, and clapped his hands. Then, with the musicians and the bridal pair at the head, the wedding party walked in solemn procession to the flagbedecked tent. Long tables were spread with steaming dishes of rice porridge, big jugs of ale, and, here and there, glasses of claret. A towershaped tart, a yard in height, graced the middle of the table, and at the upper end, in front of the bride and bridegroom, a whole flowerbed was spread out round a large flat cake, iced, with their initials on it in raspberry jam.

Villing welcomed them from the bottom of the table and said grace, and then the spoons came into play, and before long they all agreed that Maren Smeds had outdone herself. Even those who took omens from the bridal porridge had nothing to complain of to-day. The ten labourers wives to whom the waiting was entrusted, rushed about indefatigably, bearing heaped-up bowls, so that the shame of any of the guests having to tap an empty bowl with his spoon should not be theirs.

When the joints were put on the table the speeches began. First the High School director made a highly poetical oration, during which the people looked devoutly into their laps. Emanuel, who had taken off his gown, spoke next. He thanked the "Friends" for the kindness with which they had received him — a stranger — into their community, especially thanking his parents-in-law, in whose house he had found a new home. Then Anders Jörgen rose, and with a bewildered expression, stammered out some words in an inaudible voice, and sat down again. It was understood to have been a toast for the "Fatherland," and cheers broke out round the table. Later on, the weaver said a few dry words about the "New Spirit." Villing followed — as a speaker he affected the emotional line, and he called upon them in an agitated voice to drink to the "memory of the departed," more particularly alluding to Emanuel's mother. They sang a song between each speech, led by Neilsen's resounding bass.

By this time it was almost dark, and the young people were impatiently waiting in the gaily lighted hall. They were anxious to dance the bride out of the maiden state. Villing rose once again, and in burning words and amid loud cheers proposed a toast for the "People's Cause," expressing a hope that it would soon rise triumphant all over the world. Emanuel said grace and rehearsed the creed, and then the party broke up and went along to the Meeting House.

Dancing and singing were gaily kept up till broad daylight.

At midnight Emanuel and Hansine took leave, and started for their new home in a carriage decorated with flowers. All the guests gathered round to bid them farewell, and cheered them to the echo.

Shortly before, a messenger had been despatched to Veilby, as the young people there had decided at the last moment to give them a festive reception. As soon as Emanuel left the Parsonage in the morning, they set about erecting a triumphal arch over the gateway. This was to be lighted up with coloured lamps at the home-coming of the bridal pair. Besides this, they planted a row of torches at the side of the road, which cast a fantastic glare around, in the calm dark night.

When Emanuel saw the red light from the high road he caught Hansine's hand and held it fast. It looked to him as if the dark heavy mass of the Parsonage Hill were raised on pillars of fire, — and he was reminded, by the sight, of a dream which he had once had, of finding the magic word which would cause the hills to open before him...

Now he was driving with his peasant bride right into the mountain.